About Leaf Books

Leaf Books' fine and upstanding mission is to support the publication of high quality short fiction, micro-fiction and poetry by both new and established writers.

We have put over 200 authors and poets into print since our inception in 2006. Many of them have never been published before.

See our website at www.leafbooks.co.uk for news, more information about our authors, other titles and having your own work published by Leaf.

Other Leaf Books Anthologies

Available Now:

The Better Craftsman and Other Stories
The Final Theory and Other Stories
Razzamatazz and Other Poems
Outbox and Other Poems
The Light That Remains and Other Stories
Derek and More Micro-Fiction
Coffee and Chocolate
Ukraine and Other Poems
The Dogstar and Other Science Fiction Stories

Coming Soon:

The Someday Supplement

Naked Thighs and Cotton Frocks and Other Stories

First published by Leaf Books Ltd in 2007

Copyright © The Authors

www.leafbooks.co.uk

Leaf Books Ltd.
GTi Suite,
Valleys Innovation Centre,
Navigation Park,
Abercynon,
CF45 4SN

Printed by Jem
www.jem.co.uk

ISBN-10: 1-905599-40-4
ISBN-13: 978-1-905599-40-0

Contents

Introduction 7

Winner:

Naked Thighs and Cotton Frocks   Anne Shewring   13

Runner-Up:

Translations   Mark Wagstaff   23

Commended:

Jared Williams Again   Jenny Jackson   35

Looking at Water   Alan Markland   45

Turning   Pippa Goldschmidt   51

The Spirit of the Age   Nemone Thornes   63

Mortgage   Priya Sharma   79

The Volcano   Catherine Chanter   99

Like a Good Boy   Aiden O'Reilly   111

Postcards from a Previous Life   Andrew Blackman   131

You're Dead   Tom Williams   147

Introduction

Naked Thighs and Cotton Frocks and Other Short Stories contains the eleven winning entries from the Leaf Books 2007 Short Story competition.

The winning story, '**Naked Thighs and Cotton Frocks**' by **Anne Shewring**, tells of the events at the commuter station of Lincoln Hill over one hot summer. A stranger is leaving increasingly explicit photographs on the walls of the station bridge and while the travellers on the 0638 are disturbed, they cannot bring themselves to talk about this unexpected turn of events. Described by its author as 'a warning to all commuters to make sure you wear clean underwear because, in the end, you can't trust the British to be as straight laced as all that', 'Naked Thighs and Cotton Frocks' is one the most charmingly humorous slices of pertinence ever to lighten our doors.

'Sometimes,' says runner-up **Mark Wagstaff**, 'you have to wait years for a change, and what you get is not what you expect'. In his brilliant story '**Translations**', two quite different men, each facing a new life, meet on a coach stuck in motorway traffic one summer morning. As pressure builds, both are forced to confront what they want until the sudden, explosive moment when their futures are decided. The voices in this story are just dazzlingly good and the sense of tension, claustrophobia and eventual humane understanding are truly first rate.

Jenny Jackson also expertly captures an extraordinarily difficult voice in her story, '**Jared Williams Again**'. It's written in the voice of a touchingly naïve, distinctly unreliable narrator who meets a long lost childhood 'friend' of sorts whose intentions she is quite incapable of deciphering. The difference between what this young woman believes and the sinister reality apparent to the reader and to everyone else in the story is astonishingly well realised, and really very haunting.

The fourth story in the collection is '**Looking at Water**' by **Alan Markland**. It's one of a collection of stories Alan is writing in which, in his own words, he is endeavouring to engage the reader to an extent where he or she becomes, essentially, part of the process. Hemingway called it 'The Iceberg Theory' – showing only just enough of the story as will allow the readers to fill in the spaces, letting them make their own assumptions out of the author's allusions. This is an exquisite example. It's set in an orphanage in rural Australia, it's packed with imagistic little snapshots and enigmatic remembrances and it's primarily about what the reader feels it's about.

Why does Orpheus turn to look at Eurydice? That's the central question in '**Turning**' by **Pippa Goldschmidt**. Her two protagonists, Eve and Oliver, are actors playing out the myth at a Blackpool theatre, and they're getting along swimmingly until one night Oliver fails to re-enact the story. When, after the fall out, he winds up in a mysterious coma, the nurse says she can't understand why Oliver won't wake up – there is, in her words, no reason. 'What happened has nothing to do with reason,' thinks Eve.

'**The Spirit of the Age**' by **Nemone Thornes** is an atmospheric nostalgia trip and an investigation into the reliability and value of memories. In the Seventies, the story's protagonist, Alex Eliot was a star. He played Guy Cavendish, private investigator, in the hit drama series that saw him voted Sexiest Man on Television by the readers of TV Times. He remembers his five years on Cavendish as the one truly golden, wonderful period of his life. Thirty years later Alex is almost forgotten, but his co-star Ronnie Bradshaw has achieved lasting fame. When Ronnie writes his memoirs, they represent the Golden Age as something far less than wonderful, and Alex needs to know whose memory is at fault.

'**Mortgage**', says **Priya Sharma**, the author of the story by that name, is a French word that means 'death pledge'. It is also the tale of one man's obsession with the house and the mortgage that he's inherited. Struggling to meet the repayments, he is keen to accept the drastic new terms offered by his mortgage lender in this properly affecting character-driven story.

'**The Volcano**' by **Catherine Chanter** is a poignant, angst-filled tale of a boy's lonely struggle against his violent bully of a father on a ghastly week-long holiday in Italy. It's set, rather brilliantly, against a backdrop of Mount Etna – a location used to great effect as the boy comes to realise what the volcano represents to him. Dark and stirring.

In '**Like a Good Boy**' by **Aiden O'Reilly**, Stefan goes with his girlfriend to her home village for the first time. Her alcoholic uncle has stayed shut away for years in a dark room, splicing audio reels of seventies rock'n'roll. Gaunt and leathery, almost a living corpse, this ultimate bad boy exerts a strange influence on Stefan in this enigmatic story filled with memorable and extreme yet utterly believable characters.

The penultimate story, '**Postcards from a Previous Life**' by **Andrew Blackman**, sees postcards from a long-forgotten friend suddenly delivered to a group of women who now lead very different lives. The postcards rekindle powerful memories of their youth, their early loves and the dreams they've all long since lost.

The final story in the collection is '**You're Dead**' by **Tom Williams**, in which a school bully is finally expelled when a summer afternoon is revealed to be less than idyllic. It's written in the voice of a young schoolboy who witnesses an event that overrides his firmly held principle that it's wrong to tell: his solemn well-meaningness is enormously affecting, and the air of menace is palpable.

The competition was judged by the Leaf Team. Our thanks to all who entered.

The Stories

Naked Thighs and Cotton Frocks

The pictures at Lincoln Hill station first appeared during the stymied days at the tired-end of a sweltering summer. The city boiled. Evening commuters on the six thirty-eight reread their morning papers, the news already out of date, or sat listening to i-pods, their heads lolling forward in half-sleep. Those without a seat stood, melting. Fewer clothes separated the bodies. Bare arms touched and sweat-damp hands fleetingly grabbing for the same hanging straps. Naked thighs rubbed together as large ladies in short cotton frocks wriggled and tried to settle themselves on the scratchy train seats..

They are familiar strangers, these Lincoln Hill commuters: not friends, of course, not even neighbours, but they come together each day for this journeying ritual, to stand closer than all but the most loved, close enough to smell the spray in a woman's hair or to see tomorrow's stubble forming on the chin of a young articled clerk. For thirty minutes, in that crowded, heaving train, they are close, flesh-close, but strangers still.

When, on that August evening, the train pulled into Lincoln Hill, the thirty or so travellers tumbled out and began the silent, gentle jostle for a spot on the stairs. To reach the station exit and the car park, passengers need to cross the tracks via the covered wooden bridge: a flight of stairs leads up from the platform and, at the top, the bridge turns at ninety degrees. The commuters will bunch at the bottom. They will subtly move to find their space in the brief crush, climbing at the pace of the slowest, no one wanting the contact of pushing through or saying 'excuse me'.

That particular evening, Miss Taplow led the pack. She turned at a moderate pace to cross the bridge. Roger de Vancy, who was at her shoulder, heard her stifled cry as she saw the first picture. Certainly there was no avoiding it. Pinned roughly to the wall was a large black and white photograph of a penis. The picture seemed to be an enlargement from a magazine, but, as many commuters had never looked inside such publications, and certainly not Miss Taplow, they could only surmise that this was so. The penis was flaccid, which was maybe why people did not stop to stare, although two young men were heard to giggle nervously. But Captain Brian Groober returning from his job in the City put the whole thing down to kids, bored through the long summer break, and to a decline in standards generally.

The following day, the six thirty-eight travellers were greeted with a second image, similar to the first but fully erect this time, and in colour. It could have been a cutting from the same source as the first ... although, with this new, brighter male form buzzing in front of their eyes, few of the passengers could now recall that other, duller picture. Certainly it wasn't the same man: Miss Taplow noticed that at once. Years of working as a legal secretary had given her an instinct for detail.

The third day, there was no mistaking the excitement that rippled through the small crowd on seeing the new picture. Had Mr Hooper, a Systems Analyst with a major pharmaceutical company, wished to describe what he saw to his wife that evening, he may have reminded her of a certain sexual act she used to perform on him as he sat in the driver's seat of his old Toyota. However, what with the children shouting about this and that, and Mrs Hooper being distinctly groggy with a burgeoning cold, Mr Hooper declined to mention what had been depicted on the station wall.

On the fourth day, Captain Groober wondered if he should bring the matter to the attention of the authorities. Children and certainly ladies used this station. But as the pictures were always gone by the following morning, Captain Groober assumed that someone in charge was taking notice.

Friday, the fifth day, saw a whole row of male genitalia, men cut from above the hips to just below the top of the thigh, nine of them.

Then the weekend came. None of the commuters were commuting. They took their cars wherever they needed to go, filling them with dogs and children, shopping and elderly parents. Two days of fun and duty. Mostly they forgot about the pictures.

On Monday evening the weather had still not broken. The air hung heavy; the travellers were wrapped in dust and sweat. Again, they nudged and pushed each other out of the train and towards the stairs. Tina Joplin took the lead, her arms full of legal files. As she reached the top of the stairs and turned round the ninety degree bend, she let out a small but audible cry, stumbling slightly so that her folders fell to the floor, piling at her feet. The thirty or so other passengers massed around her, backing up to fill the top few stairs.

It was a new picture, but there had been a change, a new direction. It was Tina Joplin herself: young, pretty Tina Joplin. Her partner was not identifiable, his face turned away from the camera. But there was no mistaking Ms Joplin. Even out of her smart, conservative suit, there was something vaguely intimmidating about her long, active body.

Miss Taplow stooped to start retrieving the files. Alerted perhaps by Tina's cry, people pushed around, peering to look, like tourists straining to see a famous painting in a crowded gallery. They looked from the picture to Tina and back to the picture again. For a moment, Tina felt nervous, worried about judgment. She peered at the picture, moving a little closer. How shapely she seemed, how finely moulded. Gathering her files from Miss Taplow, she turned to look at the picture for one last time, smiled just a little and walked across the bridge, head erect.

The picture provider had entered a new phase, replacing the anonymous with the specific. Each day, the commuters left the six thirty-eight and mounted the stairs, increasingly eager to see who would await them. No one could say how the pictures came about. None of those featured were the sorts of people to photograph their own sexual exploits, except maybe Roger de Vancy, who did enjoy the odd visual experiment. However, Mr de Vancy, who appeared on Wednesday with a small Spanish woman he'd been tutoring in English last summer, went straight home and checked his collection. Nothing was missing and anyway, now he recalled, he'd been out of film, that tryst being a spur of the moment thing. So no naughty pictures. Except, staring at the continental curve of that Spanish breast, unarguably there were pictures.

The question of 'how' soon became a strange irrelevance. Captain Brain Groober began to lose the will to object.

Indeed, he started to feel a certain disappointment at not being featured. It was now more years that he cared to remember since he'd been with a woman. The late Mrs Groober had never viewed sex as being central to their relationship and certainly during her final, long illness it would have been ungentlemanly to insist. Now these pictures, images of real people, people whom he saw every day and who pressed themselves against him in the crowded carriage, reminded him that sex had once been a good and decent thing, not grubby at all.

The commuters still didn't speak. They absorbed each new picture without comment. Not even the photograph of Miss Wong, receptionist at Davies Barker Associates, 'Estate Agents to the City', with a middle aged woman of unidentifiable profession but seemingly abundant energy, had the power to shock. Dr Randolf-Cummings, heart surgeon at St. Jerome's Hospital, thought that perhaps he recognised the unknown lady but he saw so many people in his line of work, it was hard to be sure.

His own picture appeared at the end of the week. It harked back to an afternoon last winter when Dr Cummings had finally succeeded in seducing Nurse Clarence after a year of valiant pursuit. It crossed his mind to be concerned at the exposure the picture might bring: how would it affect his career, his marriage? But no one else had bothered, so he relaxed, noticing with some pride that other men were nodding with silent approval at the shape of Nurse Clarence's breasts and the soft dimpling of her skin. Dr Cummings felt renewed cheer, rejuvenation.

It was perhaps strange that no one saw fit to mention these goings-on to any official. Lincoln Hill was a largely unmanned station, so to raise an objection would have meant a 'phone call and the passengers had better things to do with their non-working time than harass railway officials.

Besides, things had gone a long way now. Why object to a picture of Dr Randolf-Cummings when seemingly there had been no issue about Roger de Vancy and a lady from Spain? It made no sense. And yet, some of the travellers began to wonder where this would all end.

In fact, it ended on a hot, hot evening. The sky had been heavy all day, threatening rain. The air hung thick, yearning for the downpour to begin. Commuters lurched from the train, panting for cool air. As the small crowd made its way to the steps of the bridge, Captain Groober thought that he heard music, a low, repetitive beat. He looked round, imagining it to be coming from a personal stereo some inconsiderate soul was playing too loudly. Tina Joplin, who had removed her neat royal blue jacket and slung it casually over one shoulder, heard the beats too. To Mr Hooper, the music seemed to be coming from very fabric of the bridge itself. He looked about for some speakers and then craned his neck to see if a busker was playing on the cross way. Neither was apparent. Afterwards, Dr Cummings would imagine that the music had oozed from the wooden floor, that it had poured out of the ceiling, that the bridge itself had given them this sound.

Along the cross way were thirty pictures. Seemingly, everyone was there, even Captain Groober. His picture was older and slightly moulding, but there was no doubting what he and the other boy were doing, shorts around their ankles. He looked closely, recognizing the large oaks and the river, by the old boat house. He was stunned. This picture was over fifty years old.

Miss Taplow hunted along the line of pictures, a certain desperation engulfing her. There must be something, she thought. In my forty-five years, I must have done something. When she finally saw her picture, she was amazed. It was not like the others. It was simple. She was holding the hand of a young man. Her brother. He was was tall and handsome, and, when the picture was taken, he had had two years left to live. Her own face was hardly recognisable: eager and smooth, and full of love. Suddenly, she began hearing the music again. It filled her whole body with sound, causing her to vibrate along with the rhythm. As she moved, she felt a yearning taking hold, a knot of sorrow that ripped up through her stomach and into her throat. It fought against the back of her mouth until she could hold it in no longer.

Her howl was heard above the music. It cut through the throbbing of the beat and reached out to the those moving around her. Captain Groober, still stunned by the beauty of his own youth, responded. He threw his briefcase to the floor and reached out with his arms, almost touching the shapely figure of Tina Joplin. She was now shaking her whole body, letting the primitive rhythms run through her flesh. The smart jacket dropped to the floor. As the music got louder, Miss Wong, receptionist at Davies Barker Associates, began to tear at the buttons on her blouse, ripping at the fastenings until the cloth peeled away from her body. Roger de Vancy had begun spinning, moving and turning, his arms out-stretched. He started to remove first his trousers and then his shirt so that now he twisted in just his shoes and underpants. Miss Taplow had stopped screaming, and she too began a strange dance, rippling her body as she loosened her starched summer frock. Dr Randolf-Cummings pawed at his tie and then at his shirt. He felt his mouth fill with sound, his lips opening to release a gigantic moan. Systems Analyst Mr Hooper felt his body collapsing. He tumbled forwards, his guts seeming to give way under the vibration of the moment. He swung his body away from the pictures, tearing down at his shirt, his hand rubbing across his now exposed chest.

The party danced on, each guest moving in their own world. The pulsating music seemed to have softened the very fabric of the bridge itself. The dancers moved as if on air, as if on a huge inflatable floor. Clothes were torn from flesh; hands and fingers stretched out, skimming the surface of hot skin. They whirled and shrugged, letting the music and the pictures turn their lives inside out.

And suddenly the music stopped. The wooden floor and walls seemed to shrink and harden and the air to cool. The dancers stopped too and bent to pick up clothes and retrieve possessions. No one spoke.

As the first commuters stepped from the bridge into the car park, they felt large drops of rain falling on their now cooling skin. The sky overhead was dark, the summer finally breaking. People hurried to their vehicles, straightening skirts and arranging hair as they went, and once in their cars they drove off quickly. They didn't worry about Monday. There would be no more pictures.

This weekend they could begin looking out their winter clothes.

Anne Shewring

Originally from the Wirral – the place that famously produced OMD, Glenda Jackson and Harold Wilson, although not necessarily in that order – Anne has lived in Cambridge and the USA. She currently shares a small flat in Central London with a husband and a seven-year-old son, who would like it known that he has just started piano lessons. She works as a charity fundraiser and likes children and old people – well, some of them. Many people have tried to teach her how to write well, and she is grateful to all of them. Still, the quest goes on ….

Translations

Years since I was here. Not since we were kids, me and Scott. We'd get the coach up London for the day. Hang around. Never knew I'd live here. Never knew I'd leave.

When I see nothing but bad luck to shake the treetops, that's when I think of Scott. Don't know where he went. Maybe he married some regular guy, done with the bright lights. I think it'd be nice to see him again. Wouldn't be, but I think it. He wouldn't know me, anyway; not now I'm wig and heels.

We'd get the coach to Victoria. Never know what to do. Stood in the diesel air, no clue what we'd bought for our day return. I knew. I'd bought a day with him. Would've done me fine just sat in the park, but he wanted London. Fantastic. Meant a long day. Long ride, next to him on the coach.

All these years in London, don't think I've been here once. But now I am: Victoria, gridlocked in my heart, worse than the traffic sweating up Park Lane. Got that edgy, shrunken feeling. People stare: I try to be brave. I'm not a woman, not yet. Look a trannie, a man disguised. But I won't be. Not when I get my true face.

Place still looks the same: still a bus shelter. No-one since Scott made the street an adventure, the day a treasure map. All the men who've got tired of me, tried measuring them to him; tried shaping, in my little way, their lives to an energy, harsh enough to raise life from concrete, lust from a smile on the stairs. As I've got older, as the thing that makes me dress this way, makes me this way, has hardened, I'm alone more. More Saturday night telly. More Sundays, deleting unrung numbers off my phone. Not had a boyfriend … eighteen months, two years. Don't go out. See only trannies at clinic: screwed little bundles of wonder.

People stare as I walk through, getting used to these heels. If I'd started young, when Scott went, might have made a pretty girl. At least a young one. Could've had my own hair; fresh, clear skin; no sense of hesitation. Wasn't till I wanted that I knew it was too late. Got a nice dress, nice wig, nice shoes. Forty-five year old body. When it's all done and the bruises fade, I'll be in my fifties. A woman of a certain age. Single, with cats.

Gate Thirteen. Says Gate, like an airport. Says stay inside till your coach is called. No one bothers. The glass doors wide, they're out in the hazy sun. Kids mainly: earphones and backpacks. Going up uni, maybe. There's two unis there. In the diesel fumes and burger grease, there's a scent of life beginning; a perfume, the cherry notes of a travelling morning in spring. I try to look casual, unworried, female. Like I've got holiday plans. Like one of these rings on my bony joints is somebody's safe-keeping. Like I might have a picture on my phone of a face that makes me well. I want to belong without feeling synthetic, like these kids in their cartwheeling laughter, who know their friends are their friends, who know there's always someone up for it Saturday night. Trying to look cool, I hope the wig's on proper. Try catching a glimpse in the big curved mirror as I step up.

Not been on one of these in years. Not changed much. Seats too close still. Afterthought curtains. Taste in the air of having to. Here 'cause you're skint. I need every penny. There's hard years coming. Costly days under the knife. After all the talk, the prying. All so they'd say yes.

It's busy. Sit up the back. Might need the loo. Don't want to walk past everyone. No space for my legs. Hope my bag's all right. I'd rather keep things with me. Don't like to think it's all crushed. All them kids, just got on, piling rucksacks on it. Fuck knows where they're going. When I was their age I didn't want to be seen. Didn't like going out. Just wanted to be with Scott. Handbag on the empty seat. Should keep them away. Driver's getting ready. Counting heads, checking tickets. Going anytime now. Engine's started, shuts the door; shuts London, with a swoosh of compressed air. Horn sounds as we reverse. I'm leaving.

Fuck, what's that? Someone banged the windscreen; banging on the door. Man getting on. Big man.

'Ta, pal.'

'Coulda killed you.' Driver's angry.

'S'all right, pal. You didn't.'

He fills the coach walking down the aisle. Stops the light. Big man in a black tee-shirt. He grips the seats as we swing round the corner. Knocks heads with his elbows; no one starts. He's seeing where to sit and there's only one seat left. He's staring at me. I move my handbag.

'Ta, love.'

Bounce up as he sits down, the seat inflating. He takes every scrap of space, every breath of air. There's a solid wall of him keeps me from everything. Need the toilet, soon as I'm blocked in. Got his elbow in my ribs. Got his knee against my modest calf-length sundress. Gotta look out the window. Got three hours of this.

Marble Arch and Baker Street, Swiss Cottage. Not goodbye. I'll be back, when everything's delivered. Said, in assessment, relocation to secure my mental health. To ensure robustness. That's how they see reassignment: vaccine against the future. And when I come back ….

'Eh, love.'

Why's he talking to me? Sounds northern. They talk to

strangers, don't they?

'You got a drink or something? I'm rattling.'

Got water in my bag. Just small. Don't wanna give it. But then he might be cross with me. Shit.

'Ta, love.'

He's had half the bottle. Three hours. We're not even to Scratchwood.

He's staring. Nowhere to move. Nothing but look out the window. Can't even cross my legs proper and I love crossing my legs. Breathing fast. Calm. Can't show ….

'Going Nottingham?'

Why didn't I spend on the train? Could've walked through on the train. 'Yeah.'

His eyes, big dark bolts of bloodied terracotta, going through make-up and moisturiser, through skin and bone.

I'm burning, sweat itching my scalp. He knows. Too near not to know.

'I'm going Nottingham.'

Three hours of this. Getting hyper. Breath right up in my throat. He's got me, teasing the moment till he makes me jump to his chain. This always happens. Doesn't anyone ever understand under this face I'm shy?

Taking time from the concrete beats as we hit the motorway. 'Know Nottingham, do ya?'

'No.'

'Not at all?'

He says it like there's secrets I'd do better to unravel. Mazes where you're best to keep that string tied to your wrist. Only Nottingham because I had to get out of London. Get away, get strong, for treatment to begin. The doctor asked: did I have friends anywhere I could go to? What was I meant to say? Read about places, closed my eyes, told him: Nottingham. Linen and lace and all. They helped me get a flat signed up. Showed me, on a webcam. But I don't know Nottingham at all.

Big man in black jeans. Cramped in the seat, in the moment. Tries to shuffle his knees and the bloke in front starts round. Says nothing though.

Could pretend to sleep ….

'Not been Nottingham twelve years. Long time, d'you know that?'

Can't he see I'm nothing, can't help him? Twelve years ago I was smuggling myself as straight. Thought life was more easy the less you said. 'Yeah. Long time.'

'Long stretch.' Those fucking eyes. 'You don't know Beeston?'

'No.'

'Near university. Fucking students.'

Heads bob. The laughter dips.

'Not the only place you learn lessons. Know that?'

We're slowed for traffic. Roadworks. Everyone trying to see out the front. Queue looks for miles. I'm burning.

'Fucking coaches. Can't have a fag.' Looking again, snidey-wise. 'They said to me: what d'you want? Where d'you wanna go? I said fucking Acapulco.'

We're stopped. The aircon dies. 'You got friends in Nottingham?'

'Friends?' The word's rejected as alien, repulsive. 'Got my daughter in Nottingham. And that thing, says it's her mother. You got kids?'

'No ….'

'No. Don't reckon. Going holiday?'

'Staying.'

'You're in for a treat, then.'

I'm in for a treat in London. I'm treated everywhere. We jolt forward. Stop.

'Sometimes, of a night, I'd think about this day.' He flexes his legs again. A muffled curse in front. 'You all right, pal? Good. Keep that way. I'd think, what it'd be like. What I'd do, y'know.'

I've thought about this day. Packing stuff in my little case. Chucking what don't fit.

'She's seventeen now. Young lady. Can't take her a cuddly bear for fun or a fucking Noah's Ark.'

'She'll have boyfriends.' Lucky cow.

'You what? What d'you mean?'

His breath, a hot and stale cloud. I flinch. 'Just, she's growing up, like.' Don't mean to mimic his speech. Automatic, when I'm stressed.

'You said boyfriends.'

'I …. '

'You mean she's careless? Easy?'

'No ….'

'You said ….'

'No.' Sweat muddies my foundation. Can't breathe. 'I mean nothing.'

'Fucking coaches.'

We crawl a bit and crawl a bit. Drilling fills the coach like water fills a sunk car.

'Why you going Nottingham, then?'

'Just staying.' I'm so shy.

He huffs his thick 'tache. 'In that drag?'

'I'm ….' Oh shit. Shit. Had counselling for this. But my voice betrays me. 'I'm starting to live as a woman.' Swallow the rock in my throat. 'Getting ready.'

'Ready?'

'For ….'

'To have your dick off?'

'Yeah.' Men are directing the diggers, rolling cones across, faces grimy with heat.

'Thought you'd stay London. Town's full of fairies.'

'I ….' Why tell him? 'Had to move. Problems.'

'Seen plenty. Fairies. Don't work 'case they break a nail.'

'Was you in the army, like?' Copying again. Defence from bully boys and vicious friends.

His laugh's a spit-filled bark, drives the coach to silence. 'Fucking army. If I'd been in the army, I'd have medals for what I done.' His fingers jerk in smoker's frustration. 'When d'you know, then? When you're ready?'

In counselling, we talk and talk. How I felt when I was small. How I've always had this sense of not being where I should be; of being translation, not my story but someone's telling of it. A meaning delayed, never explaining what I'm for. They believe nothing, take nothing on trust. We talk and talk for hours. They have to know you're sure. They tell you about the shit to come but I've lived that already. Tell you friends and family might struggle with the change. No worries for me. Talk through the procedures, how much it hurts, how long it takes, how deep the scars sit after. Make you know this ain't miracles but translation: different, not new; re-explained, not solved. Some can't wait, but me, I'm scared to tidy. This thing Scott claimed his hand around and made a living heaven: gone. Some shallow trough to replace it, some story that can't care. 'You feel it's time.'

'I'd fucking feel it's not.' He rubs his crotch, an angry not a sexy move. 'Seen plenty, these twelve years.'

We judder and stop again. I'm cramped, unfeminine like this. Can't find that casual way women sit like women. Nothing outside but cars and concrete. No breath but heat. Big man. Muscles, not off the gym. Useful muscles. Try pleasing. 'You must have some stories.'

'Stories? Get up when you're told. Dress how you're told.

Eat, sleep, shit what you're told. Put down when the sun's still shining. You count it in weeks. In years. Days are just ….' He gestures round. 'Just this. Cunts, waiting. Twelve fucking years. My little girl's seventeen. I missed it: school, that crap they do: the Romans, the moon. Missed it. Holidays and fucking pony club. Changing school. Her changing. What the fuck d'you think she'll say to me? Eh?'

He kicks the seat. The bloke starts up. 'Are you gonna stop doing that?'

'No, I'm fucking not, pal. I'll do it till I'm done.'

'I'm telling the driver.'

'Tell your fucking dad. If you can find her.'

There's ripples running through the seats, murmurs, cautious looks. That sense you get in a bar, just before it all kicks off. But I'm protected next to him. Not me he's come to hate. 'Arseholes, eh?'

'My downfall, love.' He checks himself. 'He was an arsehole. Him, got me put where I was. Never sly.' Sudden closeness. 'Not like these who ain't got shit till they're tooled in a gang. Faced him straight. Said, listen, pal, you and me's got business.'

'Was it accident?'

'Was it fuck. I gave him no choices. 'Ere: where's that cunt going?'

The bloke in front: he's up, spins on his heel. 'I'm going to tell the driver. Had enough getting kicked in the ribs. Had enough mouth.'

'You what?'

Big man, fills the aisle. His sudden absence opens a world of space. Relieved, I cross my legs, feeling human. There's a show for once ain't me.

'What d'you say?'

'You got some kind of problem, mate.'

'What?'

'Anger management. I ....'

We don't get his diagnosis. Don't get what observation he feels qualified to make. A gesture, a blow, a simple assault, sends his smooth face reeling. Like comedy, like the movies, he windmills back, clipping heads in baby blows of his own. Hammers the windscreen and slides like thrown spaghetti to the floor. A pesto of blood interrupts the glass.

People stare: a few lads giggle, a girl screams. Everyone gawps at the broken body, really, really not looking at the black-haired man's raised fist. In the death of conversation, the driver speaks on his radio.

The man sits down, cramps me again, but I'm grateful for his nearness. He seems tired, relieved, like he expected this and he's glad it's done. His knuckles reddened, but the colour's fading. 'Arseholes, eh?' He puts his hand on my knee and laughs. 'Bet you've had yours.'

I laugh; don't mind his pinching. It's nice getting touched.

'You doing it, then? Getting scissored?'

'We'll see. You meeting your daughter?'

'We'll see.' His smoker's fingers dance. 'Fucking coaches.'

He kicks the seat.

We pull off the M1 at Milton Keynes, not anywhere: a lay-by. There's police and an ambulance waiting. Ambulance don't need to rush. We have to get off, the coach impounded by forensics who watch too much telly. Country plods in fresh-looking stab vests, falling over themselves being busy, disappointed my big man isn't more of a fight. He's getting matey: calling them cunts like old friends. Struggling for show, he shouts me over as they tie the cuffs.

People stare as I walk through, getting used to these

heels.

'This bird,' he says, for their hearing, 'is hundred and ten percent sound. Come 'head.'

I embrace him, hot: I've never hugged a tethered man. It's electric, but sad. He's given himself no choices.

'D'you know this man?'

'Leave her out. We met on the ride.' They scoop him into the van: him kicking shins, kicking the doors. But it's pantomime, just business.

Everyone's on the coffee, waiting for the next coach. Law taking names and addresses, getting the victim's next of kin. Scott used to dress me up as a girl. It was a game we played. We had a box of pretty things: tight tops, little skirts I had the legs for then. Tall shoes. He'd dress me and say I looked beautiful, princess, urban angel. Touch me, let me imagine one day I'd come good. But he left, and I followed, always a heartbeat too late.

At Broad Marsh bus station there's somebody waiting. Some therapist, help me settle him. He'll be wondering what's kept us. Not the only one. Maybe there's some girl there, music on, dressed trendy. Keeps reading a blue-paper letter, checking her phone. Whatever we do translates into some other story. We're never the moment: just its telling, an explanation brought alive by other tongues. However good people are, however caring, it's them, not us. Autobiography is the worst deception; life is the worst truth.

We wait, complaining; everything's someone's fault. Busy here: coaches from all over. This one's heading south, back London. Leave the crowd. Doesn't take much to change direction. Not even in these heels.

Mark Wagstaff

Mark Wagstaff lives and works in London and the city provides the background to most of his stories. Mark has self-published two well-received novels, After Work and Claire, and a collection of short pieces, Blue Sunday Stories. Details at www.markwagstaff.com.

Jared Williams Again

It started again with a letter. I always look at the bottom of letters first, just to see who they're from, because they don't make any sense otherwise – you'd think people would sign letters at the top. This one started 'My dearest Shannon,' but the first thing I saw was 'Love, Jared.' After I read it, I folded it away, and I put it in the drawer. Then I watched TV for a little while before I got changed for work. And all the time I was thinking, why does Jared Williams want to come and see me?

Seven people came to my desk that afternoon, three men and four women. I told them where to sit. The phone rang seventeen times. Mr Prentice asked me – like always – if I was okay and I said – like always – 'I'm surviving, Mr Prentice.' Winnie asked if I wanted to go to the cinema with her and her boyfriend, but I said, 'No, thank you.' If I had a boyfriend, I wouldn't want Winnie to come to the cinema with us. I wouldn't even ask her.

I didn't think about the letter at work. But on the bus home I thought about it. Seeing that name brought back things I didn't want to remember, and sitting on the bus with the rain making the outside all blurry I kept thinking, Jared Williams. It's what I thought all the way home. Jared Williams.

Two days after the letter, I was watching TV on the couch. It was Saturday, and they have programmes about cooking.

When the doorbell went, he was the last person I was expecting to see.

'Shannon,' he said.

I didn't say anything at first. It's strange when you see someone for the first time in a long time. They're not the same person. Their hair's different. They're fatter. They've got lines around their eyes. All these things had happened to Jared Williams, and it took a little while to take it all in.

'It's Jared,' he said. 'Jared Williams.' He didn't need to say anything. He had Jared Williams' eyes, Jared Williams' hands. They hadn't changed at all.

'I know who you are,' I said.

'Did you get my letter?'

'I got it.'

He smiled, quickly but clearly. It only lasted a second. 'It's good to see you, Shannon.'

I looked at him. Jared Williams, standing on my doorstep. I was moving about like I wanted to pee. I already had, a little.

'Come in,' I said. And he did.

It was almost nice. We drank tea and ate cake. Jared Williams said he liked my house, even though it's a very small house, and a bit of a mess. We talked about the weather. He told me about his job, and how he was a Christian now, how he loved his church. He showed me a photograph of two little blond boys, and he told me how much he loved them, and he told me how much he missed his wife. We talked, a little bit, about his letter.

'I'm sorry I wrote to you, but I couldn't help myself.' He was sitting across the room. I usually sat in the place that was next to him, but I chose the other chair. 'I didn't want to just turn up without warning – after all these years – but seeing you in the newspaper like that, it just brought back so many memories.'

'The judge said I can keep the house,' I said.

'I know, Shannon. I read the newspaper. I'm glad.' He looked down at his empty teacup. 'And I'm really, truly sorry about your parents.'

I closed my eyes for a little bit longer than a blink, then opened them again. I do that when people who never knew my parents say they're sorry that they're dead.

'I must say I didn't understand why they were trying to take the house away from you, Shannon. I mean, look at you.' He waved his hand at me, and he looked at me with his Jared Williams eyes. 'You're perfectly capable of living here – looking after yourself – on your own.'

'I've got a job as well,' I said.

'See!' he said, beaming. 'There you go!' He put his teacup down. 'I always said that there was nothing wrong with you, Shannon. You're just not like the rest of us.' He made a little movement, and I could tell that if I'd been sitting next to him, he would have put his hand on my knee. Or maybe even my thigh. 'You're special, Shannon. A special girl.'

'I have to watch my cookery programme now,' I said.

'Of course, of course.' He stood up quickly. 'Shannon, I'm so glad I've found you. I feel like there's so many things I want to say to you. Would it be all right if I came around again, maybe one evening during the week?' His voice was the same as at school. The words were nice but he still sounded like a little boy. 'Maybe I could help you with things around the house. Or we could go out somewhere?'

'I sometimes go out with my friend.'

'Well, you could come out with me, too. Perhaps Wednesday?' He didn't wait for an answer. 'I'll look forward to chatting again then, Shannon.' He stood up, and was over to me, quick like a rat. 'Bye, Shannon,' he said, and he kissed me – soft and wet – on the cheek.

I watched him go out of the front room, and I heard the front door close, then I went upstairs into the bathroom and I took off my skirt and my knickers. They were all wet where I'd peed and while I put on some clean, dry clothes all I was thinking was that he must've seen the wet patch.

He must've known.

At work I talked to Winnie. She was really pleased that I wanted to go to the cinema on Wednesday, and we looked in the newspaper to find a good film.

'Pete'll be really pleased, Sha. He's been dying to meet you.'

I knew that they'd rather be at the cinema without me, but I smiled back anyway. I was glad that I would be out on Wednesday, that there would be only darkness behind the curtains when Jared Williams came round. Maybe he wouldn't even knock, I thought. Maybe he'd see the darkness, and think that I was out, or even that I'd moved, and that he'd lost me again. I smiled when I thought about that.

But Jared Williams didn't come round on Wednesday. He came on Tuesday instead.

I wasn't watching the TV – Tuesday isn't a good TV night – but I was sitting on the couch, just like normal, when the bell rang. I didn't think about Jared Williams until I got to the door and there he was.

'Shannon,' he said. 'Beautiful as ever.' He came in without asking me, and walked into the front room.

I followed him, and when I saw he was sat on the couch, I went to sit in the chair opposite, but he patted the place next to him. 'Come and sit next to me, Shannon.'

I was going to pee again, but I tightened all my muscles. I felt like I was going to fall over. He grabbed my wrist, and it was easier just to go in that direction.

'There,' he said when I was sitting down. 'That's better.'

I could smell him – he was leaning in towards me – and he smelt just like at school. Chewing gum. Sweat. People change what they look like, but what they smell like stays the same. 'I thought you said you were coming on Wednesday,' I said, and my voice sounded like a little girl, like little Shannon.

'Oh, change of plan,' he said. 'I'll tell you the truth, Shannon. I've waited twenty years to see you again. After Saturday, I found I couldn't wait until Wednesday.' He put his hand on my thigh. 'So here I am.'

I looked at his face, and he was smiling. I wanted to pee more than ever. 'You were nasty to me,' I said.

His hand stayed where it was. 'I was, Shannon. I know I was. But that was because of other people. Other people made me treat you like I did.' He was rubbing my thigh – little circles – and his breath was on my face. 'The other kids, they all said you were ugly – a spaz they used to say, remember – and I just joined in.' He stopped smiling. 'I thought there must be something wrong with me, Shannon. I couldn't understand why I liked you so much. Why you made me feel like you did.'

He was sitting very close to me, and I could feel how hot his body was through his shirt. 'You kissed me,' I said.

His face looked like it had stopped, like his battery had run dead. 'Oh, Shannon. You have no idea how many times I've thought about that.'

'No one else ever kissed me,' I said. I wasn't making my muscles tight now. I had that peeing feeling, but I had something else as well, something that I couldn't stop, even with my muscles.

'That's why I'm here, Shannon. Because I can't believe I only ever kissed you the once.'

'Everyone hated me. You hated me. But you kissed me.'

'Shannon, you have to understand. Little boys can be very cruel. I couldn't let people know. They would have hated me too.'

'I hated you.'

'I know, Shannon. And I'm sorry.'

I didn't know what to say. He wasn't Jared Williams. He was a man. I leant my head on his shoulder.

'Oh, Shannon,' he said. He moved his shoulder, I lifted my head, and Jared Williams kissed me again.

Upstairs, we took off our clothes, we got into bed, and we had sexual intercourse like I've seen sometimes on the TV. It hurt, and afterwards, Jared Williams cried. I tried to tell him that it was all right, that it'd hurt me as well, and that we didn't have to do it again if he didn't want to, but he got angry.

'If you tell anyone, I'll kill you.' He didn't shout. He was close to me, and he whispered.

I remembered the last time he'd kissed me, how angry he'd been afterwards, and I didn't say anything. He got changed quickly, and he went downstairs. I heard the door close. I tried to go to sleep, but I was sore.

Jared Williams was my boyfriend again.

At work the next day, I talked to Winnie. I knew that Jared Williams had said not to tell, but he didn't know Winnie.

'Shannon, are you sure? I mean this isn't just a story, is it?'

'No,' I said. 'Jared Williams was my boyfriend at school.'

'You had a boyfriend when you were at school?' she said, smiling.

'He couldn't be my real boyfriend, and everyone hated me because of what I'm like, and he only kissed me once, and he hit me when I told everyone he was my boyfriend, and he was always nasty to me.' I had to breathe. Winnie went to speak, but I stopped her. 'He found me because of my parents and the house and the newspaper, and he came round on Saturday, but we only talked, and he came round last night, and now he's my boyfriend again.'

Winnie smiled at me. It was nearly lunchtime.

'So I'm sorry,' I said, 'but I can't come to the cinema with you and Pete because Jared is coming round tonight.'

'Oh, yeah?' She was laughing. 'And what are the pair of you doing?'

I looked round, because I didn't want Mr Prentice or any of the women to hear me. 'I'll have to whisper.'

Winnie laughed, and leant her head towards me. I whispered in her ear what me and my boyfriend Jared Williams had done, and what we were going to do, but when I'd finished she wasn't smiling anymore.

Jared didn't come round on Wednesday. I watched the TV for a long time, but I turned the sound down in case I didn't hear the bell, and I opened the curtains in case he thought I was out, but he never came. I went to bed very late.

On Thursday, Winnie asked me if I'd seen my boyfriend. I didn't know what to say. She kept asking, and after a while she just gave me a hug.

I was crying.

'He's not you boyfriend, Sha. He's just a prick. If he comes round again, you phone me, right?'

'Right,' I said, and I smiled. But I knew I wouldn't phone her, and I knew Jared wouldn't come back.

That's why I went to the church.

It was a lovely Sunday morning. It was sunny, and the sky was blue, and I walked all the way. I remembered the name – St. Joseph's – because of dad's name, and I knew where it was, because I looked at a map. I like maps. They make more sense than books.

Outside the church it was very quiet. I could hear people singing, and I didn't want to go in and disturb them, so I sat on a bench next to the path. It was very hot.

When people started to come out, I watched them. They were all nice people, dressed in beautiful clothes. They all looked happy, and I started to wish that I knew how to join a church. Then I saw Jared Williams. He was wearing a suit, and he looked almost nothing like Jared Williams, but I knew it was him, because he was holding the hands of two blond little boys. They were walking on either side of him, and just next to them, holding the other hand of one of the little boys, was a woman. She was tall, thin, beautiful. She looked like she should be on TV. She was smiling, and saying something that I couldn't hear, but when she stopped talking I heard Jared Williams laugh.

They got closer to the bench, and I stood up. I wanted to pee again, but I tightened my muscles so much it felt like I was going to explode. I was shaking, but I didn't care. I wasn't going to pee myself.

Jared saw me when they were right next to me. His face almost didn't change. He was still smiling his Jared Williams smile, and he still kept holding the two little boys' hands. But he stopped laughing. The woman said something, and she laughed, but he didn't. He looked at me, then looked away, and they kept walking, and the woman kept talking. Jared Williams didn't say anything to me at all, and I just watched his back as he walked away.

When I sat back down I was thinking about when I waited for Jared Williams outside the school gates. I was thinking about all his friends, how they laughed. I was thinking about him hitting me, hard, in the side of the head. I was thinking about them all shouting at me – spaz, spaz – how I'd cried, how they'd all run away.

This time he wasn't running, and I was trying hard not to cry.

Jenny Jackson

Jenny Jackson has been writing for four years. She has had stories published online and in print in the UK, and is an active member of Alex Keegan's Bootcamp, an online writing cooperative.

Looking at Water

Rolling down the Stuart Highway, straight as a stretched-out snake, in a dust-streaked four wheel drive with the hood down, a man feels like God must feel when He gazes at what He's made. Not that she's a beauty by any means of reckoning. Red parched soil on either side. Acacia trees, cracked and broken like very old men; the ruin here and there of a silver prospector's hut. Not a live thing in sight, which is not to say that live things do not exist: they do, in legions, hidden, from which refuge they'll come and sting you. Or bite.

Mal, a tall, thin to the bone man, about forty with hair to match the colour of the soil; a brown burnt face under the regulation slouch hat and a walk on him (when you catch him out of his car) like a successful rent collector, sings as he goes along in tune to the background whap, whap, whap of tyres on tarmac. He is on the Alice side of Katherine going south.

That last job had been hard graft. His back aches with the constant stooping and the wool has irritated the skin of his hands. He has had sheep. Up to here.

Lisa Washington, he's been told, wrong side of fifty, widow, is having some trouble running the orphanage at Dolly's Creek: pop. three hundred and fifty, most of them 'originals. Maybe there's work to be had.

She's a wiry woman, Lisa; a wide straw hat against the glare and a camel's tail switch for the flies. Homespun. Outback to her core.

'Dump your kit in the bunk house,' she tells Mal, 'and you'll do.'

He can fence round the bottom end, she says, where the river slews in a tight 'S' bend; undercutting the bank so that only a sod's depth of soil remains for unwary kids to wander on.

'Don't fall in,' she cautions; 'the crocs here are really mean.'

There are a dozen children, all of them aboriginal and she brings them up with the aid of two elderly bushmen, Bill and Sol, who might have stepped out of a Sydney glossy mag advertising tourist boomerangs and from whom the kids learn the lore of their ancestors with only minimal interference from Western ways.

Mal pulls his weight, eats and sleeps well and gradually feels his way in so that, as day follows day, he becomes more of a fixture and less of the outsider. He is likeable, goes out of his way to be helpful and always has an eye out for what, if anything, is in it for him.

He still gets the dream. That other river feeding the paddy fields, stained by mud from the jungle banks beyond, by the chemical dropped from the sky above and, more than once, by the bright blood of dead or dying men. He sweats and turns as the nightmare grips him:

The girl was pregnant, or so it appeared. Heavy with another child to swell the already teeming ranks of victims. She approached the platoon, a hand held out in supplication. She muttered shrill in her own strange language. She was a mother, pleading. She bowed low. And then the horror as she straightened. The AK47 springing from the folds of her skirt, aiming at them with a defiant scream and the Sergeant yelling, 'Fire! Waste the bastard!'

Bits of her bones, blood streaked on his tunic sleeve. The smell of death, split bowels and the sweet, rotten tang of the forest.

'Shovel it in,' said the Sergeant as, for the sake of decency, they scraped what remained into a shallow hole.

Rowley is a thin boy. His arms and legs do not conform to the rest of him and his head jerks and swings at impossible angles as he walks flat-footed about the compound. He is mute. Perched every day on an abandoned termite mound, he nods and veers as Mal works at the fencing.

'You've got yourself a mate there,' Lisa tells him. 'And he don't take to folk regular.'

Mal grins at her. 'He's company,' he says, though, inside, the armour is firmly in place.

A disused water tower looms beside the gate and the fence he is creating. Holed, it stands with its rust-streaked corrugations, casting long black shadows of itself at sunset and at dawn. It is cooler in its shade and it is there that the boy sits watching, never still and always with an ear cocked for Mal's droning voice.

'You got your troubles; I can see that. But looking at me, you wouldn't think, would you, that I'm being eaten away?' The fence is coming on and the brand new palings and posts give a rejuvenated look to the whole dry landscape. Mal works steadily, stringing the singing wire between the uprights, screwing tight with the bottle screw.

He enjoys the work, gets lost in it; keeping the guilt away with a twisting of steel, the hammering of wood on wood, the keen pine smell of fresh cut timber. The sun is hot on his back and the lad brings water from the well in a pail that judders and jerks as he struggles against his lameness to walk straight.

'You never met my missus, did you, young feller? A hell cat she turned out to be, though who's to blame her nursing me?

I never meant to hurt nobody and I know before you say it that that's what they all say. I have killed, you know? Several: squeezing them out of their smoke bombed hideaways, blasting their heads off. Younger than you – fourteen? Some of them. The enemy. But you're not the enemy, are you? Pass me that bucket of nails.'

He likes to look at the water. Washed up after work and with a man's dinner down him. The swirling, rapid flow that has, over time, eroded the banking, causing tunnels into which the crocs crawl when they have a jaw full of fish or the occasional sheep that has strayed too near the edge. He would swim but for the crocs, naked like they had done in The Mekong – all those white bodies, stark against the burnt tan of their faces and lower arms. Alive, joking and some of them would be missing the next day. There'd be the service in the open air. Standing with their heads bared, listening to the words. The padre with his medals on.

'For such as it has pleased our Lord ….'

'That boy is a hundred percent since you got here – never seen him so still. How long you figure on staying?' Lisa has a frock on for a change. Handsome woman. His own age, give or take.

Mal has nearly finished the fence and tells her that perhaps he'll fix the tower if she wants to get the stuff in. New pump, valves, sheeting.

'We'll see,' he tells her.

There's been rain higher up and the river is swollen, running slower. Debris – the odd tree stump, a pile of greenery – takes a long time to float past, looking tired, reluctant, uncertain about going on. Mal turns his back on the water. Smoke is coming from the chimney on the roof of Lisa's cabin. Rowley, the boy, is in his usual spot beneath the water tower. Smiling. The fence, with a couple of weeks' more work, will enclose the whole compound. Mal will be on the inside looking out and the crocs can snap as much as they want.

He hoists the boy up onto his shoulders and walks about the stockade, viewing it from every angle. There is plenty to do here. A man could be content. They pause by Lisa's doorway. She comes out with a pitcher of lemonade. There is a misty frost rime on the glass surface. The boy touches it with a finger. A vicious spasm lashes his frail frame. And then, without hesitation, he draws a perfectly straight line from the rim of the jug to the stem.

Alan Markland

Alan Markland has been a writer since his teens but, like many others, found the demands of a working life a complete hindrance to any literary aspirations. It was only on retiring from forty years at sea that he found the time to write for magazines, in which he has been published variously. A collection of his early short stories, *Plate Pies*, has been published.

Turning

His fingers pleated the hospital sheets and his breath clouded the oxygen mask, but his eyes remained closed.

'We don't know why he doesn't wake up,' the nurse said. 'There's no reason.'

What happened has nothing to do with reason, I thought.

There are many beginnings to this story, but only one middle, and that's where it all happened. In one beginning, Orpheus falls in love with Eurydice: she dies and he goes to hell to get her back. In another, I met Oliver at the first rehearsal of this play and he sang to me. He sang before he ever spoke, and that was enough for me. He could sing the high notes and the low ones, and the sounds pushed and pulled at me. His dark hair bounced with the effort of making the notes and I could see his muscles moving under his t-shirt. It was enough. Singing is such a physical activity; it draws attention to the body. I didn't know it was a calculated effect. I thought that he was an instrument for the music surging upwards through him. I didn't realise he created it and he used it.

So he sang to me and I noticed him and the age-old question hung between us. I answered it. I helped myself to him as you would eat a pudding that was too rich, too cloying and that you knew would not do you any good. But he was luscious, so I tucked into his blue eyes and his smooth skin. What did he see in me? I once asked him, near the beginning when I was still confident that I could ask that sort of question and get a positive response.

'It's the way you hold yourself,' he said. 'You carve out a space in a room that you occupy. You're all there, all present. You're nowhere else.'

During the rehearsals of that play, in the church lit by daylight diffused through the stained glass which cast strange colours on our faces, we sang to each other. Each day I died and went to hell and he came to fetch me. But as he led me out of hell he turned to me and he lost me. Each time he disobeyed Hades and turned to face me I screamed at him to show Eurydice's anger, but secretly I was pleased. He had to turn. We were locked together like the moon and the earth.

Why does Orpheus disobey Hades and turn to look at Eurydice? The company talked about it during rehearsals.

'Because he's in love with her,' said Oliver, smiling at me, 'and he has to make sure she is following him.' I smiled back but already I was beginning to be aware of the constant texting, the whispered phone calls. I wasn't dumb. I knew what was going on. He was younger than me but his hair was already thinning in a vulnerable crest on his head. He was probably looking to settle down soon and I wasn't kidding myself that it would be with me.

'Because he doesn't trust Hades to keep to his side of the bargain.' The view of the director, who had noticed what was going on between us and seemed to be tickled by it. At least he winked at me in the pub after rehearsals when he saw Oliver take my hand.

'Because he doesn't trust Eurydice.' This was from one of the pretty girls in the chorus and I glared at her. She would sit a few seats away from us in the pub with the other pretty girls. They flirted with the lighting crew but were not above giving Oliver a lingering glance. His eyes were always ready to meet theirs, I noticed.

'Because he doesn't love Eurydice enough.' This came from Oliver's mate Rob who played the ferryman. I glared at him too. He sometimes sat with us in the pub but rarely spoke to me directly. I blew smoke in his face once to see how he'd react. He didn't say anything but shifted his chair closer to Oliver's.

Me? I liked Oliver's version, of course, but even then I could sense the flattery behind it. I think that it's because Orpheus can't do what he's told. He has to disobey Hades because that's what triggers change: that's where the genetic mutations creep in, where the cells disobey the DNA instructions. Out of disobedience comes life. If he obeyed Hades he wouldn't be human. He has to turn and the story has to go on.

I know a lot about disobedience. My name is Eve, after all. By rights, at my age, I should have had a sensible haircut, been married and divorced, and be in a nice relationship with a silver-haired gentleman who had grown-up kids. Well, I'm not. I never did what they wanted. I did what I wanted: that's why I still had long, long hair and was sleeping with Oliver, and that's why I understand why Orpheus turns around.

That was our beginning. Back then he sang at a hypnotised cockatoo in the zoo in Regent's park. He sang at the starlings in my garden who stopped feeding to listen to him. He sang at a surprised duck on the pond near my mother's house. He sang at my neighbour's parrot who imitated him. He sang at a group of schoolgirls on the tube once, and they giggled and offered him their sweets.

The beginning lasted for about a month, and then it changed. Then his eyes started to flicker over me as he sang. In the middle he sang for other reasons. He sang because he was paid to sing. He sang because he liked singing; he liked the sound of his own voice. He sang because he liked applause. He stopped looking at me and gazed past me to the place where the three pretty chorus girls stood. He looked at my costume when he sang at me. At my hair and at my make-up. Not at my eyes.

Once rehearsals finished there was no more singing just for me, because he had to keep his voice fresh for the performances. Those were the only times I heard it. The rest of the time he was quiet.

Halfway through the tour we fetched up in Blackpool. We were in separate rooms by then. He said I disturbed him at night and then he couldn't concentrate on his singing during the day. We were doing the get-in at the theatre. The costumes were being ironed, and the set was being wheeled into place. I was hanging around at the back of the auditorium in the dark, watching him at the front of the stage chatting with the hands. I was draped across two seats wondering whether to go out into the fog and try and find the tower.

He glanced towards where I was sitting but he didn't come over. I thought back to last night when we had been sitting on his narrow bed in the B&B, swigging the obligatory cheap wine.

'It's not you,' he said, 'but I find it difficult to sleep with another person. I need my own space.'

I smiled like a plaster on top of the pain, to keep it in place. He stroked my cheek with one finger, carefully, as if he was planning how to touch me.

I leant forward to kiss him. I knew he couldn't resist me really.

'Oh, Eve,' he said, but there was a sour note in his voice and he shifted away.

'Why not?' I crossed my arms over my breasts.

'I don't know.'

'Sing to me,' I suggested.

He smiled tightly. 'I can't just do it, you know. There has to be a reason.'

Singing isn't about reason. I know that.

That night as I sat in the dark space in the auditorium, cocooned in my pain, I watched him in the light. He was having fun down there, joking with Rob and the chorus girls. They were decked out in these short togas and he was pulling at one of them, as if to unravel it and expose her. The winding sheet that I emerged from in the first act was already in position at the back of the stage, looking dirty and discarded. At the beginning of the run it had been white, shining under the lights. Now it was more the colour of stale tea. It looked like a sheet that builders drape over furniture to stop things from getting dirty.

Still I stayed hidden here. The chorus girls shrieked with laughter at something that Oliver said and I watched him forensically. As he talked to the prettiest he laid a finger on her wrist. Betrayal, then, was simply a movement of the muscles. Singing is a movement of the muscles.

I burst out of the theatre and ran past the posters showing a hundred grinning clones of him with eyes as large as fists and just as hurtful. I was tearing down the street back towards B&B Land when I heard someone running behind me.

'Eve, please stop,' he panted. I stopped but I didn't turn to face him.

'What are you doing?' I asked him. 'What are you doing with her?'

'Nothing. It's nothing,' he said. But still I wouldn't turn.

'Please look at me.'

'No.'

I looked up the street, at the pub, the chip shop, the bookies. I couldn't see the sea: it was off-stage. Gulls were flying overhead. He started to sing a song from the play. It was the first song in the play, the one he sang to charm the birds and the creatures. It was supposed to charm me now.

'Bugger off,' I said over my shoulder. The gulls shrieked and flung themselves around the sky, swooping to peck at an open packet of chips on the ground.

'Please, Eve. It doesn't have to be like this.'

No, it doesn't, I thought. It can be like it was in the beginning when you looked at me and opened your eyes to me. Now they were closed. They were heavy lidded, secretive.

I finally turned, in spite of myself. I wanted to look at him, to see his eyes. But he was looking down at the birds that were pecking around his feet, trying to get at the stray chips squashed under his trainers.

'Hey, look,' he said. 'I've charmed the seagulls.'

I walked off and left him with his flock.

That night I realised that this stage was raked even more sharply than usual. Everything tilted towards the audience and nothing was true. Oliver, when he stood in front of me, was nearly a head shorter. I looked out towards the audience but I could see nothing.

The following night something happened. We were at the point in the play when I was following Orpheus out of Hades and he had been instructed not to turn around and look at me until we'd reached the surface. Except, of course, he did turn and I was lost to him for ever.

Except tonight he didn't. He obeyed Hades and just kept walking right to the top of the stage and then out through the wings. I was left there by myself. I was supposed to cry when he turned and looked at me, and then he was flung out of Hades without me. This night, I roared. The note hung heavy in the theatre, like some physical substance. It went on for too long and I realised my mouth was still open. The stage manager was watching from the wings, her mouth open too. She brought the curtain crashing down and I tore to the dressing room.

The director was in there already with Oliver. 'You prick. Why can't you leave your private life outside?' He broke off when he saw me. The dresser, another pretty girl, was looking nervous. Oliver brushed past me. The director shouted after him: 'and DON'T come back!'

I went after Oliver.

'Why didn't you turn?' I asked. He was away down the corridor towards the exit but he could hear me.

'I've introduced a new interpretation,' he said. 'I don't like the old one anymore.'

His voice was quiet and flat. I roared again and he hurried out, chased by the noise, and I was left standing in the narrow red corridor that seemed to be closing in on me. The stage manager appeared at the top of the corridor, where it led into the underbelly of the theatre, but I waved her away and went outside. I needed fresh sea air.

I was still in my winding sheet and it wasn't the best article of clothing for a windy foggy night in Blackpool, but I decided to go to the beach anyway. Years ago, when I was a teenager I came here for a dirty weekend with my first boyfriend. We had stayed in a shabby room with pale pink covers and I remembered that we had made love standing against the promenade wall. Just because it was there and because we could. What a thing to remember, I thought, and then I wondered if I could find the spot where we did it. I walked along the beach and in my mind I could still hear the note I emitted. But I couldn't tell one part of the wall from another so I sat on the pebbles and listened to them clatter beneath me.

I sat there for a long time, watching nothing. Trying to think nothing too, but not being able to stop myself from going over it again and again. When had it turned from sweet to sour? When had the fruit rotted? When had he stopped looking at me? When had he started turning away from me?

I must have fallen asleep because when I next looked at the sea something had shifted, as if a few frames of a film had been removed. The winding sheet seemed draped differently, somehow. It had unravelled and there was a seagull standing on the end of it, about ten feet away, looking at me. Its head was cocked. 'Bugger off,' I told it, and yanked the sheet around me.

When I returned to the theatre the director was waiting outside.

'Where the fuck …?' he began, and then he saw my face and said, 'It's ok. The ASM understudied.'

I was still silent. The winding sheet was dragging behind me. It had bird shit on it now, and sand marks, and something that looked like splashes of ketchup. I wanted to crawl into it and die properly this time and not be woken up again.

Instead I went back to the B&B, had a cup of cocoa and sat on the bed. It was two in the morning by now. The ASM had offered to walk me home but I didn't let her. The birds were already awake and singing but I wished they would shut up. Why couldn't there be silence?

Still my head rang from the note I had roared.

The next morning there was a knock at the door.

'Phone for you,' the landlady shouted.

It was the director. 'Eve … there's been an accident. Oliver's in hospital.'

The landlady was hovering, looking interested.

'A last minute rehearsal,' I told her as I rushed out.

But when I got to the hospital I couldn't find him. I fought my way past reception, got lost in the maze of corridors and had to climb out of a lift that jammed and disgorged me onto the wrong floor. I eventually found myself at the bottom of the hospital, where it was dim and the only light came from machines keeping people alive. I had to speak to one nurse and then another, who directed me past rooms with bodies lying in beds. Then I found him, on his back in a narrow high bed, arms flat on either side of his body and tubes in each arm. The sheets were tucked tightly in around him, binding him to the bed, like a shroud. There were strange marks on his face: sharp thin lines.

The nurse spoke behind me.

'He was found on the beach. Face down in a pool of sea water, long after the tide was out.'

'Which part of the beach?'

She looked at me closer. This was not the right question to ask.

'Up near the tower,' she replied. 'Speak to him. He needs to know you're here.'

'But I don't know what to say.'

'Sing something. That often helps.'

'I don't know how to sing. He's the singer. '

'It doesn't matter. It's your voice he needs. Even though he's in a coma he may still hear you.'

So I sang to him like the nurse suggested. The words babbled out of me like water.

But he lay there motionless so I stopped.

'It's not working,' I said.

'Keep going,' she said. 'You need to be patient.'

So I sang everything I knew, all jumbled up together. His face twitched as I sang Mozart mixed up with the Spice Girls, interwoven with Monteverdi and Take That. I was gasping, barely drawing breath, but I kept going and the nurse stood at the end of the bed, listening. I sang for what felt like hours, only pausing for sips of water every now and then. Finally I stopped. It wasn't working. Why should I carry on? Why should I drag him back here? The nurse seemed to read my mind.

'Keep going,' she said gently. 'It doesn't matter what he's done: you can sort that out later between yourselves. You just need to get him back.'

But I doubted her. And then I worried about being on the beach. What had happened in that piece of missing time? Had I seen him there? Had something happened between us? How could I not remember? In one version of the Orpheus myth, Eurydice is so angry at being left behind in Hades that she sends the Maenads to Orpheus, to destroy him. They rip him to pieces and his head floats downriver, still singing.

I pitied myself being left here without him and then I pitied him. And then I decided that there was no space for pity. I'd sung my best and it hadn't worked and so he would have to remain where he was.

'That's it,' I tell the nurse. 'I'm finished here.'

She was silent. I stood up. I looked at Oliver carefully, at the outline of his body clearly marked by the sheet. I left the room, and I didn't get lost finding my way outside.

Pippa Goldschmidt

Pippa Goldschmidt was born in London and now lives in Edinburgh, working in homelessness policy for the Scottish Government. She used to be an astronomer and still enjoys lying in the gutter, looking at the stars. She's currently a student on Glasgow University's MLitt course.

The Spirit of the Age

Sunlight and sparkling water. The harbour. Villain Number One is on the deck of his yacht. I'm on the slipway. We're talking, and he's sticking to his cover, trying to bluff it out. Just a harmless businessman, down for a little sailing. All totally innocent.

Cut away to Villain Two, walking towards us: black shades, white suit, mean expression. Then back to me – and that's such a wonderful shot; sharp focus against the blue, blue sky. The sea breeze ruffling my hair. So dark then. Such a lot of it.

Villain Two sees me, and he panics. He turns and runs, and I race after him. A close up: he's unlocking his car; he's terrified. A few shots of startled passers-by in the town, and then we're in the high-hedged lanes, with my yellow convertible gaining. That car was a character in itself. The same one through all five seasons. Total bliss to drive. Dream car.

A huge slow tractor is pulling out ahead – well, there has to be one of those. Villain Two nips past with an inch to spare. I'm trapped behind. I take a left and screech through the lanes, emerging ahead of the tractor but with the villain lost. I follow my intuition along the coast road, and there is Villain Two's car, skewed and abandoned, driver's door open.

Close shot: I'm angry and determined. That was the thing about Guy Cavendish: he was a man filled with moral outrage at least once an episode. It was always something personal.

A low-level camera and a cloud of dust, and I've squealed to a stop. Establishing shot: the bay from the top of the cliff.

A motor boat moored close to shore. Villain Two almost at the bottom of the steps to the beach. I take them three at a time. How I could run then. How I leapt about. Never gave it a moment's thought.

Villain Two wades in. Soon he's swimming for the boat – and cut to – I catch up with him, just as he reaches it. And here's the water fight ... a bit of slightly slo-mo there, spray flying ... I love this one. I just look so incredibly good. So young.

Now the villain's got his hands around my neck, but I pull myself free and punch him in the face, hard. He falls back. I've knocked him out cold: not an easy or perhaps even a possible thing to do when your feet don't touch the bottom. Villain Two floats unconscious. And there I am, treading water, breathing hard. Close up: wet, chiselled, magnificent. One hand pushes all that streaming hair out of my indigo eyes; and another case is solved by the heart-throb P.I., Cavendish.

And cue the music.

The producer, William Eccleston, told me that Evelyn's constant womanising disgusted him, and he was tired of the emotional disturbances he caused. He said he never wanted to work with Alex Evelyn again.

You bastard! Lie about the dead, why don't you? No chance of any inconvenient contradictions, then. Will never said that, I know he didn't. Maybe that's why he's left it until now to write his blasted memoirs – just waiting for poor old Will to drop off.

It's libel. Complete fabrication. Totally untrue: all of it.

Mr Ronnie British Institution Bradshaw. So loved by everyone, so fêted, so adored, with his critical credibility and his ... bloody Bafta. A man who fits these egalitarian times to perfection. Nothing grand about our Ronnie.

Nothing at all. On every chat show with his tired old tales about being dragged up in his tedious northern slum, and oh! what a wonderful poor but honest time it was. Quite happy to do his little bit of Shakespeare, and yabber on and on about the Tremendous Importance of the Art of Theatre, and then grab every rubbishy Sunday evening drama that's going, and slap on his used-up worn-out 'pity me, I'm so ugly but so very sensitive' face, and con the audience that there's something deep going on in there. Doubtless soon he'll be Sir Ronnie Bradshaw, as a reward for thirty years of lovable, cuddly, non-threatening mediocrity.

Heather's tragic death hit us all very hard. I had absolutely no wish to continue without her, and could no longer stomach the idea of working with Evelyn. Many other cast and crew members were exhausted by the difficult atmosphere he created, and also decided to leave at this point. William Eccleston then decided to bring a formal end to a show that was suddenly falling apart before his eyes.

He doesn't need to do this. He's the one with everything. Next month I'm starting in pantomime in Buxton Winter Gardens. Buxton. Pantomime ... it's not just kicking someone when he's down; it's kicking someone when he's unlikely to get up again. Ever.

Why did he do it? Why?

Sometimes they're better with the sound off. I can think about it all, without the distraction of dialogue. Remember those golden days.

My two best girls are in this one, June and Maddy, and that redhead who played a three-episode girlfriend. Guy had lots of those. Very important to him for a very short time: just long enough to be kidnapped and held hostage.

The sun is shining, as it usually was, and it's drinks on the terrace. Vodka and tonic – always Guy's drink. Mine, too. We did so much drinking, on screen and off. Not much wine; it wasn't as popular as it is now. It was the age of spirits.

Ah – there she is. The redhead. Carolyn. Carolyn Wells. She'd succumbed to my charms by the time we shot this. Not exactly a hard-fought contest. She looks good, in an icy kind of way. Hard. Highly polished. Dressed up like a worldly and possibly dangerous woman, as if there might be a knife in her stocking-top. There wasn't, as it turned out. She was a tiny bit hysterical, in the end; but it was fun at the time.

Guy and all his girls. Alex and all his girls. And in this one, no Ronnie Bradshaw. I need to remember the good times. The beach scene – I have to see the beach scene. Fast forward ….

This was June's first episode, as Lizzie: the sporty character, the outdoor girl, athletic and all-natural; so lots of racing around the court in little tennis whites, or emerging from Guy's swimming pool, sleek and smooth and wet and bikinied. She drove me absolutely crazy.

Lizzie bought the house next door, and then spent five years playing will-they won't-they with Guy. Will said it wouldn't go down well with the audience if he seemed too settled, so I flirted meaningfully with her, and with Maddy, and the answer to will they or won't they was always no, they won't. Not that life mirrored art, of course.

Ah – the beach. That beach. Guy and Lizzie on white horses, riding towards camera. That's such a wonderful shot – a touch of the Lawrence of Arabias. If I close my eyes, I'm still there. I can feel it. Cold, and the waves really crashing in. Racing down that perfect vast empty beach straight into the sun, completely dazzling, light sparking off the sea, the wind tearing through my hair – oh, I used to love riding. Love it.

I even remember what I was thinking. I was thinking about June. She was really very lovely, and she seemed interested, to say the least. So I was making plans for her, that day. Very exciting. But June turned out to be a challenge. Four and a half years!

The horses slow to a trot. Lizzie and Guy are laughing. June and Alex are laughing, too. We had such wonderful chemistry, from the beginning. It was one of the things that made the show so successful. We were marvellous together. All those evenings holed up in some hotel in Bude or Brixham or wherever, showing the rustic, astonished locals what glamour was all about. June was so good at helping me keep everyone entertained. I don't know what Ronnie means, I really don't. It was such a happy time. We all liked each other – the cast, the crew, everyone. I think it must have eaten him up just to see it. The way everyone admired me, wanted to be with me. With Alex, the star, the life and soul of that whole wonderful five-year party. I was the party. Ronnie couldn't bear it. Probably couldn't bear having a bit-part, either. Pete, Guy's nice but exceptionally dim handyman. The comic relief.

We've seen something up ahead. It's a body on the beach. Of course it is. Dead bodies constantly washed up on the beach in Cavendish country. They were as commonplace as seaweed. June's doing her best wide-eyed and fearful look: very appealing. God, she looks good. All that fresh, healthy innocence was such a turn-on.

I should have kept in touch with her. She was terribly cut up about … the way it all ended, so I heard. Well, we all were, but June most of all. She took it so badly she wouldn't even speak to me or take my calls. I did try. Then she sent that peculiar note. Please leave me alone. I never want to see you again. A strange way to end a relationship. And then I went to L.A. for all that time.

I should have tried to find her, when I came back. I did think about it, but it was almost ... embarrassing. Seeing her doing so well, while I was last year's news. Last decade's news, in fact. The price of chasing the Hollywood dream.

I wonder what did happen, with June. Why she wouldn't see me. She wouldn't agree with him. She was a wonderful friend all those years, before we finally got together. She'll remember it the way I do: the way it was. They were the best of times. The golden days. Mine. Hers. Golden days.

I've just got back. I saw June. Talked to her. For the first time in thirty years. Over thirty years.

I almost felt I was back in the show. The famous detective on a cold, dark winter night, watching a stage door in London's theatreland, with the rain pouring down. I was waiting for an age. I got drenched.

I'd tried and failed to get June's number from her agency. Guy would have sweet-talked it out of the girl in the office in moments, but I am Guy no longer. The name Alex Evelyn meant nothing to her. She wasn't even born in the days of Guy. So I wrote to June, care of the agency. A fairly desperate letter. Pleading, almost. And she did ring; she said she didn't want anything to do with me, and she put the phone down. I wrote to her again, but no reply. So I went to the theatre. I stood there waiting and watching. Getting wetter and wetter.

Eventually, a woman came out, quite an old woman. A solid, sturdy body; no shape left to speak of. A little umbrella, one of those useless folding things. No one waiting for her, no fans, no autograph hunters. I assumed she was just someone who worked there, a cleaner or something. She walked off down the alley. Then it suddenly struck me – it was June. I know what she looks like now. I've seen her often enough, on TV. I couldn't understand what the hell was the matter with me. I was expecting the young June. I'd been waiting for a slim blonde girl.

So I chased after her. The famous detective had to run, and he's not very good at that anymore.

It shocked her, seeing me. She said I looked exactly the same, that I hadn't changed a bit. She was angry, as angry as she'd sounded when she called. She still didn't want to talk. I told her it was driving me crazy, that I had to know – what Ronnie meant by it all; if he'd talked to her. I told her it had been on my mind since I read his blasted book – why she'd avoided me, then. Why she decided it was all over. Then she looked at me properly, and she said, 'No, you don't look the same, at all. You look terrible.' She gave me her address. We have a date, at the end of next week. I'm to go to see her. She said she needed a bit of time first, to adjust to the idea.

I love this episode. It's such a good one of Maddy's – she really does look wonderful. She was incredibly glamorous in real life. I think that's why William chose her. He wanted her to play herself, and she did, superbly. Georgina the gloriously false, the beautifully artificial. The sophisticated older woman – although she was a few years younger than I. Anyone over thirty was an older woman in those days.

This is the one about a missing diamond necklace and a rich family with dark secrets and – ah! – the scene on the boat. There she is – every inch the star; stretched out on a sun lounger; white beach robe, red lipstick, a scarf wound through all those soft dark curls. Cigarette in one hand, drink in the other. It was incredibly hot that day, even out on the water. She's lowering her sunglasses and giving me that look, that famous bewitching Maddy look. It's one of those flirtatious interludes. I think Georgina's just scored a point in our personal battle of the sexes. She draws on her cigarette with deep satisfaction, and lies back, luxuriating, fingertips brushing the deck.

Oh, she had such style. She was a real old-school trooper. Totally professional. No fuss, no bad temper, no hysterics. Not even when we were together, right at the beginning. We stayed good friends when it was over, all through the rest of the run. Such good friends. Some of the best times were with Maddy. It wouldn't have been the same without her. I remember that fabulous party, the wrap party at the end of season one. William really pushed the boat out. He had a huge marquee put up on the beach. She looked so beautiful. Ravishing. Some long black thing, and her diamonds, and her famous cigarette holder. We were all so beautiful then. And any excuse to dress up. It's such a shame people don't, anymore. It makes life much more enjoyable.

We walked on the beach in the moonlight. Marvellous Maddy. So sharp and witty and campy. Such tremendous fun.

When I came back from L.A., she just wasn't around anymore. Never saw her again in anything, or in real life. I should have tried to find her. I should have stayed in touch.

I'm on my way to see Maddy. Finding her wasn't easy. An entire afternoon on the telephone. It wouldn't have made exciting television.

The not terribly dashing detective, the almost elderly detective, if you want to be unkind, is driving his utterly quotidian car through the eastern hinterland of Greater London: and neither would this make wonderful TV. Sunless November. A grey city. A dead sky.

She was pleased to hear from me. She said it would be lovely to see me again, and why didn't I come down? And we talked, on the phone, and she was perfectly normal. She didn't shout, or accuse me of ruining her life. But such a surprise! What Maddy Did. And What Maddy Did Next. Three children. Three! And she said she would have liked four or five, but she started rather late. I never saw her as the sort of woman who was even remotely maternal. And now they're grown up, she's had to find something else to do, and so she's thrown herself into gardening. Gardening. Maddy. Says she loves it. Out there in all weathers, crawling about in the mud or whatever it is that gardeners do. It's not exactly Noël Coward, and Maddy was such a Cowardian sort of woman. And she's a grandmother – just recently, she said. Her first grandchild. Maddy, a grandmother.

So we talked. About her children and her new grandchild and her garden. And it didn't sound at all like the girl I used to know.

I know one shouldn't be disappointed by how people look, but I was. Maddy is fat now. Huge. Nothing left of that magnificent body. She says she doesn't care, that it was a great relief to give up the struggle to stay slim and beautiful. She never did anything else after Cavendish. That's when she left the business. Got married and settled down in the country – says it was all she ever really wanted.

She doesn't remember it quite the way I do. She said I hurt her badly at the time, when she found out about that silly fling with Carolyn Wells. Carolyn told her about it at the wrap party, the beach party. I broke up with Maddy that night. I'd forgotten that, totally. She doesn't hate me though. She talked about it as if it was all very much in the past; another life. One she felt not much fondness for at the time.

Yes, she has read The Book. And Ronnie did go to see her, when he was writing it. She thinks I'm just like him – neither of us can leave it alone, she said. The implication, of course, being that we should. I said Ronnie had made me sound like a monster, and I asked her – you don't think I was a monster, do you? She said I was a beautiful young man and a new star, and it went to my head. And she said Ronnie took it to heart, the fact that I teased him. Tremendously so. She said, 'And it was a bit more than teasing, really, wasn't it?' and just looked at me.

Ronnie told her he'd found out, while he was talking to people, writing the thing, that I'd had an affair with Heather. He'd always suspected, but he'd never been sure. I had no idea anyone knew. I was horrified. I blustered a bit, told her it wasn't an affair, and she just gave me that look again. That famous Maddy look.

Ronnie thinks I'm responsible. Responsible for what happened.

I haven't seen this for years and years. One from the last series. The terrible curse of the ancient skull. Screams in the night and ghostly apparitions, but it turns out to be someone trying to drive his wife insane. I loved the silly, spooky ones.

Guy's office. Guy and his faithful secretary, Prue, have just had a first visit from the worried wife. I'm sitting on the edge of Prue's desk. Heather's desk. How old-fashioned that room looks now. Prue's huge electric typewriter, telephones with dials, all that square brown furniture. It's a different world. And there – a lovely shot: she's looking wary, concerned. She's wearing her hair down at last. Beautiful hair. Very pale. Ash blonde, the colour of thistledown. Fine and soft.

Prue had been the modest, mousy secretary; very much in the background. In the last season, William decided to develop the character, to provide another glamorous woman for Guy to play will-they won't-they with. He told me that when we did eventually end the show, it would be nice if Guy married Prue.

Heather was twenty-three – only just twenty-three. She looks younger. She's very slim. Small and delicate. Not the typical leading lady of the time. But she was beautiful. It was just a different kind of beauty.

I can't see Heather, and ask her if Ronnie is wrong, and if it was a wonderful happy time for her, and if she has good memories of it all. Heather never had a chance to have memories of Cavendish. Even if I could, I know how she was at the end. But it can't be, can it? It couldn't be.

June found her. That's the other thing that Maddy told me. It was June who found her.

June didn't want to talk to me, didn't want to see me, and she was right. It would have been better, far better, to have left it alone. I was there for two hours, in her little flat. She told me everything. Everything she told Ronnie. She made him promise not to use it in the book.

Ronnie had guessed anyway. It seems everyone had.

The final scenes of the last ever episode of Cavendish. There I am with my two best girls, those two women who made doing that show the happiest part of my life. Maddy, whom I'd used and hurt, and who'd been putting on her brave trooper's face for four years, and June, who at the time believed all my insincere promises – and whom I'd already cheated on, twice, before Heather. And Ronnie, of course, the butt of my cruel humour. Ronnie, who hated me.

Prue has been abducted – something personal, naturally. A villain just out of jail with a grudge against Guy. We're in Guy's drawing room and we've just worked out where she's being held. The villain sent a tape recording. There were clues in the background noise. Of course there were.

June's saying something like, No you mustn't, it's much too dangerous - we should call the police, but, inevitably …

there's the yellow car, zooming off along another deserted country road. A perfect evening in high summer. Honey light. The camera tracks the car past blurring cornfields. Drama in paradise. Guy to the rescue. And there's Heather – Prue – tied up in the belltower of a derelict church.

She looks so lovely, so fragile. Hair over her shoulders, white dress all smudged and torn. This was shot after ... so she wasn't happy.

Now I'm inside the church, confronting the villain. And in a while we'll fight and a fire will start, because conflagration is the only possible ending for this type of story.

Oh, Heather. I lied to women. I used to do it all the time. Usually, my intentions were strictly dishonourable. With Heather I did an evil thing for good reasons, or so I believed. I lied to her because that morning, the morning after our one night together, I was terrified. I knew how she felt about me, and I thought, if I don't stop this now, we will get in deeper and deeper, and there will be no way out.

Heather was different – unlike any other woman I've ever known. She was innocent. Precious. Touching. Remarkable. I felt something for her I'd never felt before, for anyone, and it scared the hell out of me. I thought it might be love, and I wanted to run. I didn't mean those hideous things I said to her. I hated myself while I was saying them, but nothing else could have changed her feelings. But even that ....

I knew what they said at the inquest, at the time. Death by misadventure.

June found her, in the morning, in the hotel. She said ... she gave me a lot of details that I really didn't want to know. And she said she was near the door. The phone was off the hook. June thinks she'd been trying to phone for help, trying to get out of the room, but she was too far gone. I want to believe it. That, in the end, she didn't really want to die.

There was what they call a note. A letter. A long one. To me. It said I was the only man she'd ever loved. It said I'd made her feel cheap and used and stupid. And she'd decided that I was right when I'd called her a silly little girl. She knew she would never be clever enough or beautiful enough for me. Which was exactly what I'd said to her.

So that's how June found out that I'd betrayed her. That's why she wouldn't see me.

There was a bottle of sleeping pills too. It was almost full. June took them away. She didn't want anyone to know that she hadn't been enough for me. That I'd felt the need to do that. And she was thinking of Heather's parents, and her family. She thought if she destroyed the evidence, it would look like an accident – which it probably was. One type of accident. An accident that I made happen.

She lied to them at the inquest, about the letter and the pills. Said there was nothing there. Heather hadn't taken anything; I knew that already. It was the vodka that killed her. If you drink enough, it shuts everything down. If you're unconscious, it keeps working. Your body won't even breathe for you anymore.

I knew. But all this time, there's always been the possibility that I was wrong. I kept clinging on to the fact that Heather didn't drink, so she had no resistance to it; she didn't realise how dangerous it was. I wanted, so very much, to believe that it was nothing to do with me. But I knew. Of course I did. I think that's why I stayed in L.A. all those years, long after it was clear that it wasn't going to happen, that Hollywood would never open up. Much more sensible to have come back while there was still a chance of saving my career, while people still remembered me. But I didn't want to remember myself. I wanted to be somewhere else, someone else. Not the worthless bastard who made a very beautiful, very talented, absolutely unique young girl so devastated and so hopeless.

Ah – we're coming to the end. The villain's lost the fight and fallen to his death from the tower. A nice, clean, easy death. Heather's told me that the church is full of gelignite – he'd planned to blow my house up. I'm running through the churchyard with Heather in my arms, and I know just how much time I have before the explosion, because a hero, a man who is unafraid of life, always knows how much time he has before he needs to dive for the ground and save the girl, and himself.

Guy and Prue stand in front of the burning church, and Guy kisses her. Just a little kiss. I remember that kiss. I meant it. I'd kept thinking, after the first couple of days, that I'd made a terrible mistake, that I should tell her why I'd done it, why I'd said those horrible things; that I should try to repair the damage.

And there we are in long shot, walking across the field to the road, and the car. And then we're driving away, the fire still burning in the distance. And I was thinking, this girl has such a hold on me, I can't get her out of my mind, can't forget how she was, how she felt. So sweet, so giving, so perfect. And should I do it, should I say I'm sorry, and I was wrong, that I can't bear to lose you – and I will, I really will make the commitment, and stop behaving like a spoilt child, and let something better into my life.

And here's the aerial shot – no expense spared for the big dramatic season closer. Guy and Prue very small below in the open car, driving along the coast road, into the summer sunset – and since it turned out to be the final episode too – into a happy new life together, for ever and ever. Heather's white-blonde hair blowing in the wind.

I remember that drive, in that real car with that real girl, driving her into that real sunset. I'd forgotten we were on camera, even with the helicopter over us. I remember it as silent, just thinking, desperately. And deciding. That I was going to ask Heather to marry me, that it was what I wanted. And then thinking that I'd better be sure. It was such a big decision. Terrifying. And I needed to be certain I could change. So I thought about it, and I thought about it for another day, and another. And three days after driving that real girl into that real sunset, she was really dead.

Oh – I can't watch these things.

They don't work anymore. They don't do it.

I want to go back. All I want is to go back.

They used to take me there.

Nemone Thornes

Nemone Thornes was born in Dewsbury, West Yorkshire, and studied Philosophy at Newnham College, Cambridge. At nineteen, she sold her first short story to *The Yorkshire Post*. She wrote regularly for the Post for the following eight years. She has published non-fiction articles in newspapers and magazines, was a writer for the official Glastonbury Festival website in 2004, and was longlisted for the Alfred Bradley Award for radio drama in 2006. Under another name, she writes stories for women's magazines. Nemone lives in London and Yorkshire and, when she isn't writing, her main interest is collecting beautiful shoes.

Mortgage

I have a photograph of my grandfather with his grandfather. They're standing in front of the house. When I look at it now I can hardly believe how much it's decayed since that time when my granddad was just a boy. In the picture there are window frames, and the paint that one of us Callisters had lovingly applied at some time had only just started to peel. They had got as far as putting doors on, with hopeful hearts, and they are there in the photograph, still on their hinges, not yet warped and buckled.

Granddad's dad had died fixing the roof. Some tiles slid out from under him and he came crashing down from the height of three storeys, breaking his leg as he landed. The doctor came every week, which was more than they could afford, and it was money wasted as he didn't last long. The bone had gone through skin and made a mess of it. Gangrene. There was a time when they knew how to stop such things: long before granddad was born.

The photograph was taken soon after the gangrene got him so all that was left was a child with a serious long face and an old man. They both look stiff and straight in their best clothes, like they'd just been to his funeral. Behind them the spot where the tiles had gone is visible and when I look at it I can't help but think, Damn it, if only he'd managed to fix the bloody thing before he fell off.

Any progress that the Callisters made was undone. That was the start of the decline: of the house and our family. Once the rain gets in, you're scuppered.

I keep the photo in our bible along with the house deeds and her sale brochure. Not that I needed them. The house,

Hymear, and the debt had been in my family for so long that no-one would dare dispute it.

I'm careful not to take it out in front of Pip. I don't like her to see me looking at it. It makes her angry.

My daddy had the chance to sell it. Pip used to bathe him in the tin bath in front of the fire and listen to him patiently. Once, after she put him to bed, she asked me, 'Is it true, what Daddy said? That someone offered to buy the old place?' She never liked to call it by its name.

'Yes.'

'You never told me that.'

'It was years ago.'

'Funny. He said it was a few weeks before Carter last came for his money. Some man offering gold for it.'

I stood behind her, arms around her waist, peering over her shoulder. She was peeling potatoes, her hands deftly circling them and dropping away their whole peel in a ribbon. I've always wondered at the skill in her hands.

I stood behind her to watch her hands and feel the length of her back against me. Also, I didn't want to have to look her in the eye.

'Nah. Daddy's getting confused, pet.'

Her hands paused, white potato flesh exposed from under brown skin.

'Maybe so,' she replied.

I could hear the constriction in her throat and the way she tensed that meant she was swallowing tears. I hid my face in the nape of her neck. Of the two of us, Pip always had the greater courage.

'Well, he should have sold it, the stupid old man.' The peeling became furious. 'Here we are living in a one room shack in the shadow of that bloody ruin, working ourselves to the death for nothing, when he could have got rid of it long ago.'

The knife slipped and she dropped it in the basin. Blood stained the water, the drop spreading out in tendrils.

I turned her around and put the bleeding finger in my mouth. Daddy was asleep and the children were playing in the yard: our flock of barefoot urchins, screaming at each other as they wheeled about in wide circles.

'Why couldn't he just sell it? Jack, why?' Pip wept.

I knew why he couldn't sell it.

It was because every time he looked at it he saw the blood and toil of generations of Callisters. He saw the hope of becoming something. He remembered the stories of how the house was and of the greatness it could bring to our name. If only we could restore her. We'd have a house, a bricks and mortar house with its own deed, not a mud shack in a shanty town for penny rent. I'd inherited my father's death debt to pay, his mortgage if you want the fancy French term, but I'd also inherited a chance for greatness and Pip never understood that. She couldn't imagine us having a bedroom of our own, the children not having to sleep up under the rafters like roosting chickens. White paint and water pumped straight into the kitchen. What it was like to have soft rugs underfoot and be warm in the depths of winter.

When I was a baby, Daddy took me up there as soon as I was born, just like I did with Jamie, my eldest. As little boy he showed me the remaining tatters of wallpaper, sprigs of blue flowers on a creamy paper. Marvellous. Pip didn't understand.

What good's a piece of paper when we're starving?

I knew. I knew why my dad couldn't sell it. It was because I'd asked him not to.

Carter came again today. I like him, although Pip would put a knife in his back as soon as look at him. We could make the payment because there was work again for blasters at the quarry and Pip had taken in extra sewing. Agatha was old enough to help her now, her eyes fierce with concentration as she tacked hems.

I was cutting wood in the yard when he came walking up the path. He is younger than me and for all he has, I feel sorry for him. He can fiddle like the devil but I doubt he gets much leisure to play now his dad's dead. When Carter came up to collect on his own for the first time he was so embarrassed that he could barely look me or Daddy in the eyes. Poor lad. He can't help the role that's left him.

Carter was followed by Pleasance. His protection. I keep telling Pip we're lucky to have Carter rather than Lightfoot or Bingley, who'll happily break a few fingers if they think you're holding out on them. She won't have it though.

'Beautiful day, Jack.'

'Isn't it!'

Even at twilight the warmth of the sun lingered. Bats darted past our heads, blurs that picked up insects on the wing. Birds were bidding us goodnight as they settled down in the copse. I let my axe land in the stump, the metal edge biting the wood.

'Would you take a drink inside?'

He hesitated, well aware that Pip was none too fond of him.

'Or maybe out here on such a nice evening?' I suggested.

'That would be grand. Very kind of you.'

'Jamie, run in and get Mr Carter and Mr Pleasance a drink.'

When Jamie returned, a mug in each hand, I took them off him and told him to run along. I wanted to be sure Pip hadn't spat in them or anything.

'He's a fine boy, your Jamie. Well mannered.'

'We may live in a shed but we're still Callisters.'

'No offence intended.'

'None taken.'

I meant it. Poor Carter. He wasn't well liked. It's not a popular job, taking money from those that have none.

'How is Hymear?'

Few men know the history of the houses left round here like Carter. Hymear had been grand. A hundred acres, servants and stables to shame an Arab prince. Gardens, not just of vegetables but flowers too. All gone. My family bought it just before times changed. They'd sunk everything into it just as the bottom dropped out of easy living.

'Hymear's good.' I straightened up as much as my back would let me. 'I bought roof tile. I want to make her weather proof before winter.'

'Real tile?' He whistled. 'That costs.'

'Yes, but it's time. I can't leave it any longer.'

'Jack,' he said, and kicked the dirt at his feet. 'I hear you're blasting at the quarry again.'

'Yes.'

'That's dangerous work.'

'It's not for long. Just until winter so I can finish the roof and cover the payments.'

I hadn't meant to embarrass him but he flushed and turned back to Hymear. The sun was behind her making her a black shadow on the red sky. I'd boarded up her doors and windows and tried to patch the roof. It made me feel better to look at her.

'It's a money pit.' The voice came from behind us.

'Shut it, Pleasance.'

That was the closest I ever heard Carter to being harsh

with anyone. Even Pleasance looked surprised. He was a brute of a man, whoring and gambling his money away like a fool.

'I'll make something of this place. And I'll pay off the mortgage, or at least as much as I can, so that Pip and Jamie and the little ones will have a proper home and something for their children and their children after that.'

I held my chin a little higher. Carter looked touched.

'All right. I was only saying.' Pleasance sounded like a peevish old woman. 'No need to get all narky.'

Carter walked up towards Hymear, waving Pleasance away. The lummox sat on a log and oiled his sword.

'Tell me what you've got planned.'

'Her foundation's still sound and the walls are still good but she needs a bit of repair. Once the roof's sorted I can start on the floorboards and the staircases. There's a man in Fallowfield that makes old window frames.'

'Hymear is a lifetime of work.'

'It's my life. She'll be a proper home.'

'Pip would say that you've got a proper home now.'

That made me uncomfortable.

'Why are you chasing this so hard?'

'You of all people should know not to ask me that.'

'Just think about it. You're one of the last few. No-one keeps these places anymore. They sell them or pack up and leave.'

'Some do.'

'Rich men, Jack. Not rich because of their houses but rich to start with. Selling Hymear would set you up. The interest you'll pay in your lifetime would buy you a nice bit of land down on the flats and a herd for grazing. '

'That's why I can't give it up now. We've put so much into this. I can't throw it all away.'

Carter put his hands in his pockets. 'What if I said I can help you?'

'What do you mean?'

'What if I said I could reduce the interest rate?'

'Why would you do that?'

He looked uncomfortable, like the first day he came up here with his ailing dad. I'd just got married then.

'I don't want you getting angry. Forget what I said about the interest. I'll waive it. Anything you give me would be off Hymear herself.'

'You're crazy.'

He didn't look crazy.

'I want Jamie.'

I nearly hit him. I was glad I'd left my axe down in the yard.

'Hear me out,' he said. 'Jenny and I, we've not been blessed with a child. And you have so many ….'

'Yes, so I can gift one anyway like a pup from a litter!'

Pleasance stood up and ran to us, but Carter motioned at him like a shepherd to his dog and then pointed at the log.

'Listen to me.' Carter was all reason. 'All I mean is for the boy to live with us. You're his father. You'd see him all the time. You could get Hymear sorted and be moved in by next year. Even if she's a shell, she'll still be sound and dry. Can you imagine Jamie bringing a wife back here when he's older?'

That made me listen.

'Why would you do this?'

'A man with no elders has no past. Without children he has no future. We have no future, Jack. We can give Jamie something, an education. A chance. Otherwise he'll end up stuck here, slaving away to that wreck of a house.'

'Like me, you mean.'

'No!' He threw down his hat. It was a strange day. 'You're obstinate, Jack Callister! I'm just trying to do you a good turn and look how I get treated.'

After a moment I picked up his hat and passed it to him. 'Here.'

He was flushed. I never knew that Carter had such passion in him.

'Let me think on it. I'm not making any promises though.'

He held out his hand to me and I shook it.

'That's all I ask.'

We sleep on the pallet I built. The children are up in the loft. Before Daddy died, he was down here with us, over by the fire. Pip never complained about the lack of privacy. She's good like that.

I could hear her breathing. Lying on my back, with my arms behind my head, she slept on my chest, one arm and leg thrown across me. I'd planned to forget Carter's proposal. It was ridiculous. But I couldn't sleep and the less I slept the less ridiculous it seemed. Jamie was bright. He'd do well with a bit of schooling and if Carter was happy to pay for it, then Jamie could go far. Where that boy gets his brains from I don't know but they missed a generation with me. I reckon it was from Daddy. Jamie has a look that reminds me of him.

What Carter said stuck in me like a shard of quarry stone. When Jamie is married. What a gift to him. A house for all the Callisters. A whole generation under one roof, with most of their death debt clear.

We would still see Jamie in church. He'd visit. We'd make him understand that it was for the best.

I could see Hymear near complete in my lifetime.

Pip raised her head a fraction. 'Why aren't you asleep?'
'Just thinking.'
She leant up on one elbow, all her hair trailing down. 'What about?'
'Don't sound so surprised. I can think as well as you.'
'I know that. What's wrong?'
There would never be a good time to tell her.

Afterwards she sat up, her back to me. I understood that Pip's silences bear an iller wind than any rages or tears. She picked up her shift and pulled it over her head. It's hard to be angry at someone when you're naked.

'Did you suggest this?'
'No. Carter did.'
She fell silent again. My little wife with her big anger, bigger than any man I've ever known.
'When?'
'It would only be if we wanted. We could wait a while, talk about it.'
'No. I meant when did he ask you?'
'Does it matter?'
'Yes.'
'Last week.'
'And you've only just decided to tell me?'
I shrugged. She lit an oil lamp.
'Come outside. We'll wake the children.'

Moths fluttered around us, excited by the light. My thin breeches thin didn't keep out the cold but I didn't dare go back in for my trousers. Despite her bare feet, she didn't seem to feel the chill.

'Jack, sell the house.'
'No-one will buy it.'
'We need to start again. Sell it and we can get away from here, from Carter and mortgages and wet nursing other

people's babies. From the quarry and me worrying that one day they'll have to fetch me back what's left of you from under the rubble.'

'He wouldn't be taking Jamie from us, love.'

She rounded on me. Instead of firecrackers she was softly spoken. 'Is this what you really want? For our son to go away and live with strangers? I love you, Jack. I honestly love you, but please don't do this. I've done everything you asked of me, but please, not this.'

I held her face in my hands. 'We'd be giving him everything. An education. Property. And it wouldn't just be for him, it would be for all of us. The girls would find it easier to get husbands. We'd have a place to grow old in.'

'We'll find a way. We don't have to take Carter's charity. I'll take in more work.'

'You said yourself: how much more can we do? We're barely denting the interest.'

'I don't know how much more I can do, Jack.'

'Hush now, darling. That's why we have to do this.'

'No, you don't understand.' She gave me a half-hearted shove on the chest but I pulled her back to me. She was crying and making no sense, each thing she said at odds with the other until finally she was at the nub of it. 'I'm pregnant again, Jack. We're going to have another baby.'

Jamie cried when Carter and Jenny came to take him away. Pip didn't. She just stood by the fire, hands crossed over her swollen belly. She looked the picture of calm when only an hour before she had been a whirlwind, dusting and sweeping. She sent Agatha for flowers to put in the china jug Daddy bought us for a wedding gift. She dressed the children in their best.

Jenny was fine enough but no beauty like Pip. Why Pip

fell for a man like me, I don't know, when she could have had her pick. I swore then that one day she'd have a good dress, like Jenny's. My poor Pip, who never asks for anything.

We made small talk and poured the fresh tea that we'd saved for special occasions. The silence was heavy and cumbersome. I told the children to go outside and play in case they suffocated under it. I envied them, running around in the sunshine while we sat in darkness. I could hear them laughing.

My necktie was choking me.

We lapsed into silence again, uncertain of how to proceed. Finally it got too much for Jenny, who blurted out, 'We'll give him the best of everything. And we'll love him like he was our own, but never forget he's yours. We understand that.' She took a big gulp of tea before she continued. 'We'd never try to take him from you. He's your son and he's a real credit to you both. I'm just so grateful that you've let us be part of his life.'

She drained her cup, thirsty for motherhood where Pip was all but drowning in it.

Carter leant forward, addressing Pip. 'This must be all right with you. I won't take him unless you agree.'

Pip's lips stretched into a colourless line. She nodded, a curt jerk of the head. He was showing her respect and that was the best she could do.

'That's settled then.' Carter went to the door, a shadow in the bright strip of light. 'Jamie, lad, come here.'

I made great progress through the rest of the year. The same money was going out on materials and to Carter but it was different. It was as though a burden had been lifted. I took on extra work at the quarry and when I came home, dirty and tired, Pip wouldn't say a word; she;d just help me to strip down and fill the tin bath for me. She picked the stone splinters from blasting out of my back. She became quieter, which I took to be the tiredness of pregnancy.

We finished the roof. It seemed a patch job compared to the original but it was still cause for celebration. I sat on the step with Frankie and Will, the boys I'd hired to help me, and we supped ale.

Carter and Jenny brought Jamie up to see. I waved him in and he stood on the porch with his hat in his hands. My little boy that I was always telling to stop running and shouting had become serious and still, wearing buckled shoes and his hair curled, the same way Carter wore his.

After church each Sunday, Jenny sent Jamie back with us to spend a few hours. Pip would question him about his week: what he ate, what he'd learnt at his studies and what Carter and Jenny had said or done. She never seemed satisfied. Once, when he brought back some boiled sugar sweets for the children, I thought she would near explode.

I was working on the inside of the house now. At night I'd come home and replace floorboards. I had found a man in Arondale who specialised in old-fashioned staircases. When the cold set in Pip wanted to move in but I persuaded her against it, saying the flues needed clearing so we could light fires. I wanted to do as much as I could, so when she finally unpacked the trunk there she'd be amazed.

We had another son, Christopher. Pip became wet nurse to a child from Darry Mills. The children helped tend the vegetable plot and somehow we managed.

Jamie grew with speed. He'd be a tall man but slight compared to me. What pleased me most was his quickness of mind. I didn't like it so much when Carter started to teach him his business. He'd walk side by side with Carter, hands behind him, copying Carter. They would walk up the hill, deep in conversation about compound interest, with Pleasance trailing behind them.

Instead of waiting outside, Carter would now come in. He was the picture of manners but Jamie seemed ill at ease. It was as though he was seeing us with new eyes, given to him by Carter, and Jamie didn't like it. He winced as I ate my pie with my fingers and I could see him watching the babies in the yard, their feet muddy, when not so long ago that was him. At church he'd sit between Jenny and Carter, now looking ahead where once Jenny had to tell him to be still because he'd always be looking about for us.

Pip saw it, being quicker than me. At first she didn't say much, fussing over him in her normal way. I thought it just that he was growing up and sometimes boys get funny at these times.

'Jamie, I've been thinking,' Pip began and I wondered what she'd been thinking that she could not say to me first. It was a Sunday and she had boiled a ham. 'Maybe you should come back and be with us.'

His jaw stopped working.

'It's not right, Jamie, for a family to be apart like this.'

'Pip, let's not be hasty now.' I wished she had talked this through with me first.

She drew herself up as she dished out another helping for him. 'I've not been hasty. I've given this a lot of thought. I want Jamie to come home.'

Jamie put down his cutlery. 'I don't want to.' His voice was quiet, where before he would have shouted to be heard above the others.

'What?'

'Pardon, Ma. The word is pardon. And I don't want to, thank you very much.'

That near stopped me dead. Big as he was, Pip would

take him over her knee and give him a whipping he would never forget.

'You ungrateful little sod! Get out. Get out of here and never come back, do you hear me?' She flung the door open. 'Go back to Carter and his fancy ways, you little turncoat!' All the colour had gone from her face and she quivered as she spoke.

Jamie got up, pausing to push his chair under the table.

'Never mind that. Go.'

He stood for a moment and stared at her with a boldness I've never had. Then he left. I followed him out of the door and down the path. I put a hand on his shoulder to comfort him. 'Jamie, don't worry: she'll calm down. You know what a temper she has.'

He threw a look of disdain over his shoulder as he walked away. He was his mother's son, after all. His eyes were Pip's. I was caught between two clashing rocks and crushed as he disappeared among the trees.

'Go outside and play.'

The children looked up at me from the table, their bowls still full.

'Now.'

Pip sat back on her stool and as they looked to her for approval, I shouted, 'Am I or am I not master in my own home?'

There was a scurry of little legs as the room cleared. The food made slopping sounds as Pip tipped it back into the pot. I watched her, trying to be calm.

'We can't afford to make Carter angry. We'll never get a better deal than this.'

Pip was gripping her end of the table so hard that her knuckled blanched.

'Is that what this is about? That bloody house?'

'That bloody house has been in my family for five generations. I will fix it! I will make it a home again! All this time I've been working like a slave to make it right for you!' My fist banged the table with each sentence.

'Oh no, don't you dare. Don't you go and blame me. Don't pretend that this has been for me or the children. This is about you. It's always been about you and that house. If it were up to me we would have blown the thing to hell long ago.'

The baby was crying. Pip picked him up, cradling him close to her, a hand on the back of his delicate head.

'There now, Christopher, it's all right. Ssshh.'

'I will clear the mortgage.'

'At what cost?' She rocked Christopher to quieten him, her voice a hiss. 'You've already sold away Jamie.'

I reached for my coat. 'When he's a man he'll understand. He'll be proud of our name.'

'Where are you going?'

'To talk to Carter. I'll not lose it all because of this.'

She barred my way. 'No, you'll not. You'll not go to him, cap in hand.'

'Carter will hear this from Jamie. Maybe if I talk to him I can make this right.'

'Don't you dare.'

'Why not?'

I've never laid a finger on Pip in all my life. She is a strong woman, in spirit, not size, and would hit me with a frying pan for my trouble, but my blood was up. With Christopher still in her arms, I grabbed the back of her neck in one hand and inches from her face I shouted again, 'Why not?'

'Because Jamie's Carter's son, Jack. Jamie's his.'

I ran away from her. If I'd stayed with my hand on her neck I would have snapped it. Pip threw herself against me, trying to stop me. 'I was young. We were both so young, Jack. It was before we wed. That was the only time, I swear. I love you, Jack.' I couldn't make my mouth form the questions so they stayed there, in my head as I ran. She must have known she was pregnant. Oh, the artful things a woman can do to trap a man. I was at the point of fever when she would be suddenly coy. Pip must have been relieved at finding a dolt who would fall happily onto one knee and propose.

To think I'd been relieved to find she was happy to have a quick ceremony and satisfaction rather than a long courtship and an expensive wedding day. I thought she was as mad for me as I was for her and didn't want to wait.

Had Carter known all along? Is that why he shuffled his feet and took my money with his head hung? They must have been laughing together, him and Pip, knowing that.

No, I knew that to be wrong. Pip could barely look at him.

Oh God, Pip could barely look at him.

At that I finally cried.

From high on the hill I could see the house below me. Hymear's new orange tiles looked garish against the worn bricks. I'd made a gaudy whore of her, painting on bright colours that only served to cheapen her. She sickened me.

Running blindly, I fell and twisted my ankle. I could feel my boot-laces swelling as I hobbled on but the madness in me made me observe it from a distance. Low tree branches whipped at my face.

It was the Sabbath, so the quarry was empty. It was a gaping hole in the earth. I wanted to gouge out a similar one in my chest. I wanted to excavate my heart and toss it away so the pain would stop.

I took my key from my jacket. If I hadn't carried it in my pocket, my resolve might have faltered. I might have gone back home and Pip might have persuaded me to stay.

I carried the sticks back with care. I lined them up in a carry crate, swaddled in straw. The journey back was no headlong flight but each step a careful one. I had no intention of dying.

It was getting dark so Pip couldn't see me up on the hill. I laid the sticks of dynamite with care, running the fuses well out to the shelter of the trees. The shack was distant enough to keep them safe.

Only a true blaster understands it's not the noise you make that predicts the effects. I'd set the dynamite along supporting beams, at the base of weight-bearing walls and deep in the cellar so that Hymear's foundations would be shattered. There was a series of bangs.

I was in that moment when the action has been taken and the course is set and you wait for the consequences. There was silence, a pause in which she reproached me, and then the telltale sounds of imminent collapse. Hymear was rumbling, deep in her bowels, like she had indigestion.

I didn't think I could feel any worse until she started to creak and groan. I covered my ears. Bricks swayed and toppled as she caved inwards. Beams collapsed and tiles slid from the roof, shattering as they landed. I thought of grandfather's daddy on his ladder.

Pip was screaming my name.

The air was filling with dust. The wind had picked up Hymear and carried her to me. I could feel her on my face. She was the grit in my eyes. She was in my ears, in my mouth. I breathed her in and breathed her out, knowing it was for the last time.

I have a photograph of grandfather with his grandfather. They're standing in front of the house. When I look at it now I can hardly believe how much it's decayed from that time when my grandpappy was just a boy. In the picture there are window frames; the paint that one of us Callisters had lovingly applied at some time had only just started to peel. They had got as far as putting doors on, with hopeful hearts, and they are there in the photograph, still on their hinges, not yet warped and buckled.

It's a marvel that once such a place existed.

I have my photograph and my deed, along with the brochure of sale. I'm careful not to take it out in front of Pip. I don't like her to see me looking at it.

Priya Sharma

Priya Sharma lives and works as a GP on the Wirral. Her short stories have also appeared in *Libbon, Twisted Tongue* and *Dark Tales* magazine.

The Volcano

Scars of humiliation were burning onto his cheeks. He fumbled, trying to fit the empty juice carton in the unused plastic coffee cup, but that pushed the spoon onto the floor and he couldn't pick that up without putting the table away and getting up – but the fasten seat belt sign was illuminated. He felt the oxygen draining from his lungs and the pressurised cabin imploding around him.

'Come on! Thomas! Pass the rubbish,' growled his father, before turning with deceptive jocularity to the air hostess. 'He wouldn't need to train as a pilot. He's got his head stuck in the clouds the whole time anyway.'

His father. The holder of the branding irons.

'Makes it look as though we don't know the first thing about flying.' Keith spat the words at his wife as the hostess glided on to the next row.

The father was in the aisle seat, with easiest access to the drinks. The mother was in the middle, which was where she always was and would always need to be. Thomas had the window seat and could now see the coastline.

20,000 feet beneath him, arid ridges of mountains looked like a 3D relief map he had seen at the Science Museum. He could make out tiny villages clinging to hilltops and dry riverbeds on valley floors. Occasional features broke the vastness: a shrunken reservoir, a motionless windfarm, a motorway linking town with town. And in each town, invisible people, going to work, going to school. And in each school, invisible children looking at the clock waiting to go home. And in each home, invisible boys, in front of their fathers.

Then, far in the distance, like a diagram from a textbook,

was the perfect triangular formation of a volcano. Thomas stared at this great, puffing dragon of a mountain; he looked around, hoping to share the excitement but there was no-one available to him. He contained himself. Etna!

As it turned out, he could not only see Etna from the window of the plane, but Etna could see him on the balcony of his room. The holiday company wouldn't allow him to share his parents' room now he was over twelve. Keith had complained because of the cost, but Thomas knew his mother had other reasons for wanting him on a camp bed in the corner; reasons she would not name but which felt big to him and frightening. So here he was, a deserter, a freedom fighter, a child soldier in his own room. He could hear them through the wall, opening and closing cupboards, turning on the television. Quietly, he locked the interconnecting door.

Etna and the boy stared at each other over the valley floor. The sun was slowly setting behind the mountain, making the jagged rocks at the summit shine like gold teeth. The sky and sea had merged into an intangible pink haze reminding him of the soft incense in the catholic church where his mum took him at Easter; the lights on the lower slopes of the volcano flickering like the candles on the altar. The slow twilight wove its way around the town, gathering up families, bringing them together to eat beneath the shadow of Etna. Thomas could make out a faint glow running down the slopes of the volcano. He stared into the breeding darkness, allowing the features of the nighttime face of the mountain to become clear until he saw that the craggy, uncommunicative blackness was broken by a strange seam running down one side of its cheek. The glow brightened until he could make out a puce steaming scar that dug into the skin, revealing the bone and teeming fluids beneath the surface. A molten streak of lava was spewing from the crater. To Thomas it seemed to carve a graffiti message on the side of the mountain.

The lava flow was primeval but it spoke to the boy in the language of violence and raw power that was familiar to him.

Loud banging on the door made him jump. The hatred he felt for his father oozed out through his sweating palms as he struggled to get a grip on the handle.

Keith wanted to know why he hadn't unpacked.

'I was looking at the volcano,' offered Thomas, avoiding what would inevitably become a lecture on his sloppiness. 'It's amazing!'

'Well, it's been there for the last thousand years and it'll still be there when you've unpacked,' replied his father.

Thomas unpacked in three minutes. Shorts and tee-shirts in the chest of drawers. Books and disposable camera by the bed. Washbag in the bathroom. What was all the fuss about? But that was always the question with his father, wasn't it? What was it all about?

Hanging behind them, on the way to the dining room, he looked at the artists' impressions of Etna that lined the lurid corridor. Some were like a child's drawing, with simple triangular lines and swirling smoke at the top. Others were bleak, showing the volcano covered in snow. How could the ice could conceal? Another presented the volcano as the background to the warm security of the Mediterranean village, with fishing boats and people drinking in cafés. Had he drawn Etna today it would have been vast and red and everything else, for thousands and thousands of miles, would have been indescribably small and unsafe.

In the mornings, Thomas and his mother were marched to the pool. Keith walked ahead like a mountain ape, his skimpy trunks bulging. His body was tanned: he took on the outdoor jobs when the weather was good and left the kitchen fittings until the autumn. If indoor jobs did come up in the summer, he gave them to 'the lads' as he called them. He was proud of having lads of his own. Proper lads – just like he'd known in the army. He said he'd been happy then and it was true that he looked like he was smiling in the photos. Andrea followed in her new bikini and her new black eye; the former covered by an Indian wrap that tied at the back and the latter covered by her overlarge sunglasses. And then there was Thomas. Beneath his baggy shorts he thought his pale ankles looked like joints from the skeleton in the biology lab. Fear of the feeble orange hair in his armpits and between his legs stopped him swimming. Against these tanned and laughing teenagers in the pool, he felt himself a freak.

The mother sunbathed on her front, hiding her face; his father propped up the bar, drowning his disappointments. Thomas stayed out of the pool: the week looked interminable, but the tourist information he was reading suggested one thing that could make it all worth while. An excursion to Etna.

Price 80 Euros. Book early. Thursdays only.

Three problems then. Price. He couldn't imagine that his father would pay. Book early. That probably meant today. Even at breakfast this morning he had heard other families talking to the Rep, signing up for coach tours. And Thursdays only. Today was Monday. They left again on Sunday.

He wanted to do this trip more than anything he had ever wanted to do before.

After lunch, a heavy silence fell on the hot still water. The laughter of two children in the toddlers' pool sounded as though it came from another country. The bell from the church tower in town tolled three and in the distance Etna sent silent signals into the blinding sky to mock him. Thomas sat in the shade, his knees up to his chest, returning the challenge.

'Amazing, isn't it?'

Thomas squinted up and saw the Rep. He agreed with her. She asked if his family were going on the trip on Thursday. Thomas looked quickly at the rising and falling flab of his father's beer gut. He was an expert in rapid risk assessment. It was safe to continue.

'Is there a reduction for children?' he queried.

The Rep thought for a second and replied that there was a family ticket, but that probably wasn't much help, was it. No, it wasn't.

'Am I allowed to join the trip on my own? I am nearly fourteen,' he lied.

She promised to get back to him and later that day confirmed that he could go. She wanted to know if she should put his name down.

'No' said Thomas.

'Yes,' said Andrea. 'If that's what you want, then, for once, I'm going to make sure it happens,' his mother had said. 'Trust me' – that's what she had said. Trust me.

Lunch didn't bode well for any future negotiations about the trip. They were sharing a table with a family who had three of the sorts of boys that Thomas should have been.

He stabbed at the white chicken, dead on his plate. The worship of other people's boys was a religion for his father: in fact he was the great high priest of other people's sons. Thomas' face was burning and not from the sun. So much anger was forcing itself up through his thin throat that he could not force the food down.

'You need to tell our Thomas that he'll never make the team eating girl's portions,' mocked his father. 'What's that? Speak up?'

Thomas drew his head up and stared straight ahead. 'I said I don't care if I don't make the team.' Each monosyllabic word was paced and pronounced in a breaking voice and with vicious precision. His mother flinched at his unexpected bravery.

'Don't care? Don't care was made to care; don't care was hung. Don't care was put in a pot and boiled till he was done. That's what we used to say in my day.' And Keith's laugh was too loud and everyone else's laugh was too quiet. The heat was building in the claustrophobic dining room; someone was pushing more sound, more light, more heat, more needles into his head until it could contain no more, no more pressure. No part of him, not his food, nor his clothes, nor his books, nor his dreams, no part of him was left intact by the shredding of this father. No more shredding. There would be no more shredding.

Out of the best of intentions, out of the need to reclaim small talk and safe turf, the mother was chatting about a teenagers' games day, to take place on the Thursday.

'Then that's Thursday sorted for you, young man,' said Keith. 'Sign him up.'

Thomas followed them back to their room after lunch. He had made up his mind.

'What the hell you doing in here?' shouted Keith, pissing like an elephant in the en suite. 'I paid enough for you to have your own room and keep out of my way. Poncing around making me look like an idiot.'

Thomas looked out at Etna, towering above him, above the hotel, above Keith.

'I'm busy on Thursday,' he announced.

Keith came out of the bathroom, doing up his flies. Thomas kept his back to him. Andrea hovered between them, folding her towel over and over again.

'I didn't quite catch what you said, Thomas.'

'I said,' he repeated clearly, 'I said I am busy on Thursday. So I will not be able to take part in the competition, even if I wanted to.'

'And what exactly are we doing on Thursday?' sneered Keith.

Andrea intervened. She plunged into the churning violence, protecting, protesting, pleading that Thomas could go on the volcano trip. Lying that Aidan's dad had kindly said he could go along with them. Exaggerating that they had even offered to pay. Said Aidan would like the company. Prostituting herself for peace when she suggested that Thomas' absence would even 'give us a bit of time to ourselves,' nudge nudge. Wink hit. Slap kick.

Thomas hated to see her selling herself like that. Sweet talking and lying just so that he could go out for the day. He lay rigid on his bed next door waiting for the raised voices and the sobbing. The eruption of this foul-mouthed ugly man who called himself his Dad. He stayed in his room for the afternoon, crouched on the floor in the dark corner behind the television, initially cutting the brochure into a million pieces, then cutting himself.

He had no option but to join them for dinner. Aidan's family and the other family were sitting together, so there was no room for them. Thomas knew the pattern. Families often sat with them once, when they were on holiday. Then they sat on their own. Boiling humiliation showed in the creeping crimson in Keith's face. Everyone who came in paused for that split second and looked round the restaurant at who was sitting where. Sit here, Thomas prayed, sit here and rescue us. But none of them did. In the end it was the Rep who broke the silence when Keith beckoned her over.

'Hello, love,' leered Keith. 'We've something to tell you. Now, Thomas here is called Thomas for a reason, aren't you, son?'

Thomas looked at his mother. It was not a new joke.

'Doubting Thomas from the moment he was born. Always changing his mind. So, if it's alright with you, he'd like to back out of the trip to this volcano tomorrow. When he signed up he hadn't heard about the games and that's much more his cup of tea. Isn't it, Thomas?'

Thomas looked at his mother. His mother's eyes were hidden by her sunglasses. His father looked at the Rep who looked at her shoes. That's what people usually did – look at their shoes. And she took her clipboard and crossed his name off the list for the trip to Etna. He had been erased.

His room darkened and outside the sun slowly sank behind the volcano. He was aware something had changed. There was no longer white smoke rising quietly from the dome; rather, three vents were stirring like vast engines, spewing great clouds of smoke into the blackening sky. Clods of ash in ill-formed shifting shapes of eyes and claws hung heavily above the mountain and obscured the ability to see beyond it. The long red scar had thrown the daylight pretence aside and throbbed once more in the darkness, the raw outward mark of Etna's violence, nourished by a perpetual stream of white hot lava, fed by invisible sources of deep tumult.

Thomas understood what it was trying to say to him. The scar revealed the true nature of the volcano and it was done that way so that everyone, even in the darkness, should know what lies beneath and should not be fooled by its daytime demonstrations of light entertainment. And he knew what he wanted to do.

Thomas washed, cleaned his teeth and then took the bathroom glass in his hand and weighed it. He undressed completely and turned off the air conditioning in his room. He needed to feel the heat. Standing at the balcony, the dogs barking in the town below, he curled his toes on the hot concrete and felt his body swell and the tender gashes on his upper arm throb. The unspoilt moon hung in the sky like the child he used to be. Somewhere, a baby crying was comforted by an unseen hand, and settled back to sleep.

He walked back into the bathroom and closed the door. He put on his flip-flops to protect his feet. He smashed the glass onto the white floor tiles. Methodically, he squatted and used the towel to sweep up the glinting glass into a corner, then picked through the pieces like a monkey sorting those things that were useful for survival and those which were not. He selected one long shard that was curved and smooth at one end so that it sat neatly in his hand. He touched the sharp point of the other end with the index finger of his left hand until a tiny drop of blood appeared on his skin. He watched it bubble. He did not lick it. He stood up and looked at himself in the mirror. He was not small, creeping like an insect, like an intruder, like a skinny schoolboy. No. He was tall like a mountain, straight like a soldier and look – see how strong he is now, opening the interconnecting door.

The shape of his mother, curled like a foetus, is just visible to him. She is facing away from Keith, as always, and her hair is covering her eyes. He feels her sleeping fear and, for the first time, despises her for it. Trust me was what she had said. Keith, his father, his f-ing father, lies on his back, naked. Although he is dormant, his snores are wet and guttural and irregular. He farts; he heaves. Thomas stands by the bed.

He raises his right hand, clutching the shard of glass, and places the pointed end a fraction away from the puce skin beneath the heavy eyes. Keith does not flinch. With a steady hand and a calm mind, Thomas draws the shard violently and irrevocably down the pitted surface of his father's cheek, carving a scar that is deep and red and angry.

So that people will not look at their shoes. So that everyone will know what lies beneath.

Catherine Chanter

Catherine Chanter grew up in the West Country and went on to study English at St Anne's College, Oxford. After several years as a lobbyist in the UK and abroad, she retrained as a teacher, specialising in supporting children with behavioural difficulties. She currently works at The Tavistock in London. Catherine has had several short stories published and written for BBC Radio 4, but her passion, both in terms of reading and writing, is poetry.

Like a Good Boy

Children swung from the bars of the frame. Their voices were small and hard like pebbles. Even the smallest ones clambered up the metal ladder and were fearless of sliding down. Their legs and arms were nut brown from the sun. Summer had started early; there had been a full month of such weather.

In the city he came from such a ramshackle climbing frame would have long been cordoned off. The sandpit too would be closed for safety reasons. It might conceal dog shit and children could pick up diseases.

Mothers and grandmothers sat on the bench and smoked. They ignored the children's tireless squabbles. A mess of cigarette butts had accumulated at their feet. The sandy loam continued to where the children played, and backwards from the bench to the steps of the blocks. The pit where the children played was a zone of deeper, cleaner sand.

'Aunt,' said Anna, 'can we leave these upstairs?'

'Is it yourself?' squealed the woman in delight. 'Who is the young man you have?' Anna flapped her hands impatiently.

'Stefan. You'll meet him tomorrow.'

'Do you have the Holy Communion presents?'

'It's all ready. Is there anyone upstairs to let us in?'

The aunt leaned back her head. 'Just himself.'

'How is he?'

'Sitting up above, recording away.'

Stefan pushed open the sheet-iron door and let Anna in first. The steps were bare and gritty. The walls had a smooth finish with the appearance of salami in greytone. They bounded up the stairs, glad of the cool air.

Anna knocked at number 462. A leathery face peered

out. Eyes sunken in, teeth exposed in a grimace. Thin lips worked soundlessly for a couple of seconds. 'Anna,' he blurted. 'You're back.'

'I'm often back, Uncle Bartek.' She pushed ahead to the kitchen and unpacked the bouquets and presents. Bartek followed her, his mouth hanging open. He walked with carefully-placed steps, not feebly, but the walk of someone who does not trust the ground. Then he noticed Stefan.

'Take a seat. I'll get you coffee, sit down.' The room they entered was a black cavern. Heavy curtains hung over the windows. The air caught at Stefan's throat. His tongue felt sticky. He tasted cigarette tar. 'Don't mind the things there.' A pair of long scissors and something like a box of medical equipment lay on the table.

'You develop your own photographs?' asked Stefan.

'Which? No. That's audio tape.' The thin man seemed pleased at the mistake. 'See?' he said and unwound a strip from a reel.

Stefan's eyes adjusted to the dark. He made out stacks of glass-fronted cabinets. Row upon row of labelled boxes. Audio reels, each labelled and dated. He flopped down on the low couch. The long open box held several instruments of dull-grey surgical steel. Aged but flawless.

'Do you see how this thing can splice the tape? Do you see the angle it cuts at?' Bartek leaned over. Stefan caught the whiff of a deviant body chemistry. An inorganic smell that shrivelled his stomach to a knot.

'Uncle,' said Anna, 'where is Monika?'

Bartek stared hard at her a moment. His lips struggled, perhaps forcing back a curse. When he spoke it was in a subdued tone. 'She plays in the playground all day, as far as I know.'

'Oh Jesus – she was one of the girls on the swings and

I didn't even notice.' Anna put her hand to her mouth. 'I think I was looking straight at her.'

'This is the tweezer – German production – and this the guillotine, and this is masking glue.'

'You have the old style audio reels.'

'That's it. High fidelity.'

'Uncle. This is Stefan. Will I make some coffee?'

'Stefan … oh yes. I believe you lived abroad for a while?'

'I was in London for five years.'

'Dead right to get the hell out of here. Me? I'm too far gone now. Nobody wants to employ a living skeleton.' He rose up, gaunt and leathery. Sucked in a breath through his nostrils. 'I can't offer you a beer. I don't keep any in the house. One whiff of alcohol and an inner battle begins.' He held his ribs. 'Sometimes I cannot even walk past a shop where beer is sold. I take a walk the odd time to get air. At night though, when they are all closed.' He gave a nod towards the kitchen and lowered his voice. 'It's a shame that I cannot drink a beer with you. If I was a decent uncle, me and you, we'd get blasted drunk together so I could see what kind of person you really are. That's the way we do it here.'

He sat again, resumed splicing the tape. His mouth smacked dryly in concentration.

Jestadaj, the labels said. Yesterday. Stefan walked along the cabinets reading dates in the dim light. 1971 – 1976, not a month missing. The longhand script was meticulous. Strokes of ink leached shadows of red and orange. With every step a sick feeling in his stomach intensified.

'Jestadaj,' Stefan read aloud.

Bartek took up the song in a tuneless chant. 'All my troubles seemed so faw away. Now a need a place to hide my way.' He sprang up and opened a cabinet. 'Bay City Rollers, do you know these?'

'Yes. I only want to be with you.'

'Yes, yes. Now you have it. Gilbert O'Sullivan?'

He shook his head.

'You don't know Gilbert O'Sullivan?'

'No.'

'I told you once before and I won't tell you no more get down get down get down.' He stamped the floor viciously on the last three beats.

'Where did you get all this music?'

'I recorded it from the longwave radio. The authorities wouldn't have liked that. The evil influence from the west. Creeping into our innocent little country like the Colorado beetle.' He took down a squat jar, set it flat on the table. He eased the lid around and it came loose in the palm of his hand. A thick black liquid lay within.

A wild idea ran through Stefan: this was the drug that kept him alive, kept those jaws moving, muscles twitching, long after the body should have turned soft and decayed.

'You'll have one too?' Bartek took out a pouch and rolling papers. The life-breath whistled hoarsely in his nose as he tapped and rolled. It took concentration to keep his fingers from trembling. His tongue searched for enough moisture to seal the cigarette. They both sat back on the couch. Stefan rolled the smoke in his mouth and inhaled lightly. Bartek sucked and hissed at it, his dry lips unable to form a seal around the cigarette. The tip at last glowed and kindled.

'I dip them in here when they're finished.' He indicated the jar of tarry liquid.

Stefan had given up smoking years before for the good of his health. But such concerns were remote, almost shameful to mention. He looked at the dark wall. A framed photograph of three long-haired young men. They lounged against a shop entrance, big sneering grins. He did not recognise Bartek directly, only by eliminating the other two. They too were the damned. He did not know what they were doing now, but knew enough not to ask.

'Do you go out much?'

'It's as much as I can do to go to the shops. I get dizzy in the heat of the sun. The doctor said …' – and here he jumped up again, as he did frequently during the visit – '… he cannot understand the nature of my physical organism. He says he measured my blood pressure and sugar levels and I should be dead twice over. One drop more, he said, will kill me. And I believe this. I truly believe this.' His eyes challenged Stefan to refute him. 'When I came back I drank sixteen cups of coffee a day. I needed to have something going into my blood to keep me steady. They gave me tablets at the clinic. But I pushed them away. I didn't battle alcohol to get addicted to these. Keep the little white tablets. They're only a sedative, she said. No, keep the damn things, I said.'

'When was this?'

The man counted in his head. 'Fifteen years ago. More.'

A noise came from the kitchen.

'You and Anna, hey? You like her, yeah?' Stefan snorted in reply. 'You'll be happy with her. Not a beauty queen, but she's got a nice body, short and stocky. That's the best kind. And she's been well brought up.' Bartek crossed himself, from forehead to stomach level, left to right shoulder. 'Nominen bominen bubblegum bubblegum,' he said. 'It's a great world when you can believe the priest at mass. Stick to the home and the church and you can be happy in a place like this.'

'It's been a while since I was in a church,' said Stefan.

'You've been abroad.' The way he said it, the word held some of the meaning it used to have – the West, freedom, the real world outside. 'Tell me, you've seen the candles. Do other places have this fucked-up religious psychosis?'

He had seen the candles. Stretched out along Ulica Marcinska for five kilometres. Normal street lighting had been turned off. No light came from any business or shop; just the glow from thousands of lanterns. The smell of wax rendered the air itself sacrosanct. It had been like that in every town and city for three days.

'You'll be happy,' he assured Stefan again. Anna was in the hallway now, turning the bolt. 'You're not the type to cause trouble. I bet you're a good boy with her, holding back the urges. Know what I mean? Yeah I can see that: you're one to get a good job and not make life difficult.'

The sun shone on the concrete slabs. Green weeds strayed up through the joints. In another month they would be baked away by the sun. A drift of sand lined the new tarmac road. The slabs, the blocks, the road too all looked as though they had been set haphazardly on a shallow bed of sand.

He approached her slowly, not knowing if this was the goodbye scene. But she was jumping with impatience and he reflected that maybe last night was not as significant as he had thought. It made him happy to see her in good humour and he broke into a jog.

'Quick,' she said, grabbing his arm.

'Why did you wait outside? I would have gone up to collect you.' He took off his jacket and loosened his tie. It was not hot, but soon would be.

'I don't want my family fussing over you.'

'Oh, the family,' he mocked. He wound his free arm around her, pressing her backwards.

'We have to go.' She wriggled. Then fell limp; let him have his way. 'That's my mother over there.'

A small round woman stood opposite with hands on hips,

dressed like a peasant, long skirt and scarf. 'Oh my God,' she squealed, and ran inside.

'Will you get into trouble?' he asked.

'Don't mind her,' said Anna. Bells rang out. It was a thin, dislocated sound. 'Come on, we have to hurry. Jesus, I don't even know where it is.'

She clutched her things and ran straight-legged across the tarmac. In this part of town the apartment blocks stood haphazardly around. Wide spaces stretched between them.

'Are you sure it's this way?' The sound seemed to him to come from a different direction.

'How should I know? It's a new church.'

'It's your town. I say we go this way.' They walked and ran in spurts. A low circular building lay off the road ahead of them, surrounded by tilled land. Cars had pulled up outside. Some drivers, with no sense of decorum, had driven right up to the doors.

'Asha is my only cousin. We didn't know each other at all as children. I remember meeting her at confirmation or something, but that was all. She didn't go to the same school. Somebody asked me once, that Asha, she's your cousin, isn't she? And I said, Nooo, I don't think sooo. I was embarrassed that I didn't know her, that was all. I was afraid she might ask me something about her. And just imagine that person went straight back and told Asha and then her mother knew and she said never speak to those people again. So I used to see someone like her in the street and think hmmm, maybe that's her, but she doesn't look like someone who's just had a baby. She probably doesn't recognise me any more. I grew up quickly. For a while. People said they didn't know me.'

Anna spoke rapidly. He found it hard to follow her sometimes.

'But you got to know each other?'

'Oh yes. I jumped out at her and said, you're my cousin. Straight away we got on well. She's just like me. Same fashion, same way we laugh at mad things. But a different physical shape.' She closed one eye and traced a curved outline with her finger. The woman standing before them now tilted her head, made a pretend frown.

'This is my favourite cousin, Asha. Asha, this is Stefan.'

'Pleased to meet you.' Asha wore a dull brown bodice with criss-crossed strings drawn in a knot. She looked wholesome.

'We're late,' Anna remembered. She ran the last few yards to the church, heels clacking up the steps.

They filed along the pews. Each clasped something in the hand: Stefan his jacket, Anna her handbag, Asha her décolletage. They sat bolt upright and prepared their minds for an hour of blankness.

Children stood patiently in the aisle, swaying perceptibly. 'Child psychologists agree,' the priest said, 'that the age of criminal responsibility begins around eight years. Though you may teach these children, they are not a product of that teaching. What is the nothing out of which a child creates a conscience?' These were strange words for a priest. Stefan looked up to check for the white collar. He tried to follow the sermon, if it was the sermon, for he was not sure what stage of the mass they had come in at. But the words seemed to fall back to traditional priestly matters. The woodcut stations of the cross, stained glass windows, smoke from incense imposed their own discipline. He woke from this to realise it was still the homily and there was at least an hour left to go.

One child turned his head, grinning and inviting others to grin with him at this outlandish garb. Never been in a church before, Stefan could see: looks delighted at the whole dungeons and demons atmosphere.

One of them was hers. Maybe even this one.

The thought made him queasy, the profane secret hidden at the heart of the world. He eyed her sideways, this Asha, the tied cleavage she wasn't thinking about, the country garb she wore. She looked like any girl who might catch his eye in a bar. There was nothing to suggest another person had come out of her, all those years ago when he had been repeating his school certificate, never as much as pummelled a girl's ass in his hand. He would have been the type to snicker when she walked past in the yard. Could she tell that when she shook his hand?

Anna on his left tugged at his elbow. Time to kneel. She joined her hands and bent her head forward. Her genuine fervour shocked him. During the six weeks he'd known her there had been nothing to suggest this. Perplexed, he fell to his knees alongside. As he did so, his abraded penis caught in his underwear and he winced.

The previous evening they had gone to the sports bar. This was a flat-roofed building built to be a changing room for bathers at the lake. A gully ran down the centre of the room. It didn't feel right to get drunk in a place of hard tiled surfaces. Three old men stood by the door and drank their beers. It was perhaps more comfortable than sitting on the steel chairs.

'Here is where me and the girls used to sit. We spent all the last year of school here, every night. Then I passed the exams and never came back. The barman asked one time, Where's the spiky-haired girl with the, and he trailed a strand of hair between his eyes, like I always used to have. Will she ever be back, he asked.'

She was happy for him to see these places that now felt

like relics of the past. He too thought back six years: a noisy disco night, a gaggle of girls at tables and just one among many he could have got to know, though of course he didn't really know her yet.

They stumbled through the woods surrounding the lake. It was another secret place. He tripped her up and let her fall on top of him. Twigs and briar ground into his back. She didn't get off him and he moved his hands over her. Lights from the street filtered through the trees. He knew that from the bright road nothing could be seen in the pitch black forest. But it is hard to believe in one's own invisibility. He backed her up against a tree, both trying to find a foothold on the bulbous roots. People walked home from the bar on the road outside, talking in loud voices.

They waited until no-one was on the road before emerging. The undergrowth caught at their feet, scratching and stabbing their ankles.

'So this is where the town girls bring their boyfriends,' he said.

It was the wrong thing to say.

'Do you think I take boys in the woods to fuck?'

'No,' he said.

'Do you thing it's my habit to take boys in among the trees to make them spew?' Her face was pinched together in hatred. She walked on ahead of him. He jogged up alongside. She swerved so as not to see his face, walked with straight steps, seeing nothing but the path at her feet.

'I didn't know what I was saying,' he tried.

'You bastard. You could have said something to make me happy. And instead you come up with the most horrible thing.'

She cried all the way home. He felt exposed; people would see them. A stranger in town, a sobbing local girl. This was the end of the road. He had not thought that words could have such an effect. He had not meant anything. It felt trite to just say sorry. Like putting a penny in the right slot.

He caught up with her again at her doorstep. She faced him, letting him see her tears, the wrong he had done her. 'Say something,' she said. 'Say something that would make me happy.'

And so he did.

The children craned their necks to see the action: two priests blessing a basket of loaves. And now the procession came down the aisle at a stately pace. A loaf was handed to each child, who kissed it and held it forward with horizontal forearms: a pose more iconic than the modern paintings in the alcoves. The new church could not yet afford statues. A teacher passed along, keeping order in the lines. Close to the end now, Stefan thought to himself. He took a deep breath and glanced around for a window to look through. He was thinking the same thing again half an hour later when the priest was reading out a list of those to thank: the parents, the flower arrangers, the bakers, the choir.

It was over. Anna bent over to exchange whispers with one of the communion girls in long satin robes. The girl was brimming with excitement, her braided rope flailed out. Her fingers dug into the thin crust of the loaf. She tripped inside her long robe, two and a half steps to every one of Anna's.

'This is the most cleverest and sexiest girl you'll ever meet,' said Anna.

The girl squirmed in giggles.

'And she had to memorise pages of things for today.'

The girl took a rolled sheet from her sleeve and handed it to him. She looked nothing like Asha.

'And her name is Monika.'

'Hi, Monika.'

'Say something funny to Monika.'

The garden was already full when they got there. The church was too small to hold everyone. Guests milled about from table to table. A few men stood under the eaves closely observing the activity. They had the look of people waiting for their chance to come. From time to time one offered to help the women carry out the trays of food. Wide boards of shaped melon with strawberries and kiwis, plates of cold meats, white sausage, gherkins, chicken drumsticks.

Then a screech of excitement: the communion girl, dragged her by the hand to meet the grandmother. Stefan felt his hand firmly gripped. He was thinking of the mother's behaviour that morning. He felt hemmed in by the tables, the handclasp, the cluttered trays of food, and the men standing so still and pointlessly against the wall. Though he hadn't eaten breakfast he was not at all hungry.

'This is my grandmother. She has all her wits about her, and isn't doddery at all yet,' said Anna.

The old woman placed her hands on his shoulders so he had to stoop. Hunker down, Stefan, like a good boy. She asked him where he was from. She told him she had lived there for five years, that the people there were nice people and that they could be trusted. Stefan gritted his teeth, nodded sincerely.

There was no beer or vodka on the tables; it was not that type of occasion. He chose some cold cuts on a plate for himself. 'Whow,' he breathed out. It was meant to indicate how hot it was. Asha smiled at him and tightened the lowest string on her décolleté. He rolled his eyes to show how ridiculous an idea it was that he would be looking at her cleavage.

Time for photographs: Asha and Anna under the cherry blossom, little Monika between them. 'Wait,' Asha said, running to pick up an axe that was lying outside the woodshed. Monika squealed and struggled to escape. Asha held her by the shoulder and poised with the axe aloft. Cameras snapped, people chuckled uneasily, a voice called out for a proper pose.

The mixture of roast meats and exotic fruits was intoxicating enough for Stefan. Some of the men sneaked out and came back to stand by the shed with bottles of beer behind them on the windowsill. He was offered one, but didn't accept. It was all right for them, but perhaps not for him.

'What was the axe for?' he asked Asha. Music was playing.

'What?' she said and leaned forward. With a slow movement he reached down and tightened her front strings. 'My goodness,' she laughed, flinching back at last, 'you'll have to watch yourself.'

He picked up a slice of melon, panicking at the thought that the daughter was her daughter, and he really had forgotten the connection. Her brown eyes mocked him, as though forgiving him a boyish joke.

'Have you ever been abroad?' He sought a random exit from the situation.

Anna came back, and the two women were soon laughing about the old days, growing up apart as kids, and a place called the cellar.

'Her father is such a madman. You wouldn't believe it. He used to pour methylated spirits through a loaf of bread and squeeze out the alcohol. So one morning he went to the local shop and said, "a loaf of bread please". The shopkeeper narrowed her eyes at him. "What do you want it for? Your good wife bought bread at eight this morning, why do you want bread at this hour?" And she threw him out like a stray dog.

'So he went to the cosmetics kiosk and says, "Good morning madam. A bottle of Przemyslaw aftershave, please." And the lady moves the packages and looks him in the eye. "I know your type," she says. "A half-litre of aftershave, eh? And you with a wife and child." And Bartek throws up his hands. "Jesus fuck. No bread, no aftershave? I'm going for a beer."'

The chair legs squeaked across the boards. 'Steady on,' he said, and pushed the mass of female limbs back into position.

A hand clutched at the tablecloth and tugged it in spasms. 'No bread, no aftershave,' Anna squealed again. 'God, he was a laugh.'

'And what was that about the cellar?'

'When Asha was little Bartek went mad and chased them round the kitchen with an axe. "Parasites," he roared. "You're sucking the life from me." Asha and her mother ran out of the house and down to the cellar. Later, when he was asleep, they sneaked back and took mattresses and blankets with them, and set up house in the basement. They threw out the old junk he had there and made it nice and comfortable. Set up a bed on several logs, brought down a radio.'

'It was so embarrassing to go to the shops,' Asha smiled. 'They used to give me extra food. I wanted to stay in all day and hide. We lived off instant soups.'

'And meanwhile "the lord of the realm" roamed freely in the three rooms upstairs, playing music at maximum volume day and night and night and day.'

'Bartek,' Asha explained, 'had dreams of being a star. He ran a rock 'n' roll radio station for three days, until the police drove up and took away the equipment. The three days of being a radio star went to his head. He was never the same after that. He used to write letters to foreign DJ's, even to the bands themselves in England and America. There was never any reply. Those bastards have me on their files, he used to say.'

'More likely the British radio stations had him on their files. Warning: Don't answer this Polish nutter.'

'That explains the audio tape,' said Stefan. 'He's still a big music fan. I know more about music than anyone else in this godforsaken village, that's what he said to me.'

'He probably does,' conceded Asha.

'The maestro of the absolutest crappiest seventies hits,' said Anna.

'Will he be along later?'

Asha looked at him, puzzled. Was this a joke that has gone over her head?

'Invite Bartek?' said Anna. 'You mean, the Bartek we were just talking about? Are you mad? He'd drink the water from the flower vases.'

'Nobody here would speak to him,' said Asha. 'He hasn't left the room in years.'

'But he is well remembered,' laughed Anna.

Stefan laughed too. He had tried to think things back into the domain of the normal. That all things were, at the back of it all, ordinary. But they weren't. In a room on the fourth floor the dead man sits at a table splicing reels. Nobody here pretended it was otherwise. Blood like creosote. Preserved beyond his time. He'd make a good corpse, laid out straight in a coffin of the same colour. A fine noble corpse.

He looked with mixed admiration at this ruthless woman, incredibly a year younger than him in years. She smiled at him, a patronising smile to one who could never understand the intensity of her life, a mocking smile to one who will touch with fingertips and withdraw from the burn.

'Monikoo, show Uncle Stefan your presents.' The chubby little communion girl trotted over. He followed her into the house, down a corridor to a newly-furnished room. She showed him her set of beads made from milky purple amethyst stone.

'How much money did you make today?' he asked. She was momentarily shocked, waited for a sign that this was a joke.

'I'm only keeping a hundred and giving the rest to mama.'

'You're a good girl. A hundred is enough for anyone.'

'It's loads of money,' she agreed. 'Have you got one of these?' She showed him a pocket games machine.

'No. I couldn't afford one.'

Monika looked pleased at this. She was an ordinary plausible kid, he thought, just like Anna in fact. He didn't think at all of her mother when talking to her. And it was good so.

The girl went back out to the yard. He poured a jug of water in the kitchen. It was as warm and humid as May can get. The promised rain had not arrived. 'Asha,' he said to the cupboard. She had given herself to some sneering local fuckwit who probably boasted to his mates over a bottle of mocne. And he at that age would have been the one to listen in and snigger. Afraid to look any good-looking girl in the eye.

Six years in London had changed him. He felt himself above village taboos. The child made no difference to him: she was a nice kid, that was all. He was ready to bear the consequences. His was the kingly power. He had seen what he wanted and was worthy of it now. She thought herself beyond touch because of the child. She had learned to despise the small-town admirers.

She walked past. He blew her a kiss.

'Asha. It's good to see you.'

'Anna was wondering where you were.'

'Anna is a nice girl.'

'I'm sure she is,' she laughed. 'You already got some water? Better take some glasses too.' Her bare arms stretched past him to get some. He passed his hand around her, lightly, so she turned to him, a puzzled look on her face. Their bodies shifted off balance, crushed against each other.

Then a dizzying crack to his jaw. Tears clouded his vision and he stumbled back thinking, that noise, that was me being hit. And then he thought, that was no slap, that was a punch, and to his amazement he's on the floor and she's not there. He feels shame: under an evil influence he had attempted to take sexual advantage of a young mother. No, he is shocked: the violence bred into her has reared its head. There were no borders to what she was capable of. Or no: she had only intended to slap him, but the glass was in her hand. Perhaps she hadn't noticed the glass in her hand. All possibilities are equal; there is no starting point to think about what has happened, no reason, no proportion. She was nice to hug.

A sharp pain shot vertically up his cheekbone. He realised now why it is named the eyetooth. Realised too that those who have been chased to the basement by a man with an axe do not know the bounds of normality.

He got up, staggered for the bathroom. In the corridor he saw the front door open and thought, briefly, about leaving. He splashed water into his mouth and spat; gargled and spat several times but the water still ran red. His heart was pumping too hard; the blood flowed too fast. Holding back his head, he cooled his forehead with a wet cloth. Slowly he reasoned back to normality. She had hit him with a heavy water tumbler. No teeth were broken, only a bit loose. No sirens were wailing, for him, or for her; no women were screaming.

He waited as long as he safely could before he would be missed, freshened his face one last time in the cool water.

'Tooth infection. Flared up on me again,' he mumbled his way past a couple of the remaining guests. At the end table three pairs of eyes watched him, awaiting his next move. He had no idea what they were thinking.

Aiden O'Reilly

Aiden O'Reilly is from Dublin, but has lived most of his adult life abroad, in London, then Berlin, and later in Poland. Since his return he has become more active in trying to get his work to an audience. This was difficult in 2004 as Ireland's main literary magazine went bust and the second one took indefinite leave. Since then, he have been lucky enough to live to see new outlets for his work appear. In March 2006 his stories appeared in Ireland's two main literary magazines, and in July a story was included in the anthology *These Are Our Lives*. In 2007 his work has appeared in *3am* magazine and *Arabesques Review*.

Postcards from a Previous Life

The first postcard arrived while Olivia was making breakfast for the children. She hadn't noticed it at the time: the flimsy sliver of colour wedged between the gas bill and the ominous-looking notice from the council. But later, when the children were at school and the brief solitude of mid-morning was settling around her, she scanned through the pile of letters again and noticed the postcard.

From California. A picture of sun, blue-grey sea, curvy road hugging a craggy coastline. 'Monterey' shimmering in bold red letters against an impossibly blue sky. The faint tickle of envy that sunny postcards always gave her on grey Cricklewood mornings.

She flipped it over to see who it was from. The girlish purple-inked script with the tails of the letters curled impishly upward and the 'i's dotted with hearts stopped her instantly. Her mind slipped a gear. Cricklewood, California, Liverpool, the kitchen table, student rooms, kids, the smell of marijuana, coffee, PTA meetings, vodka tonics in the college bar.

She slipped the card back between the magazine offers, her heart beating a little too wildly. 'You really must take it easy,' she could hear her doctor saying, as if that were possible with three children and a failing marriage. And now a postcard from Sharon dropping into her life, pretending that it was still 1987 and they were still writing cute little cards to each other with curls and hearts, talking about holidays and boys, utterly oblivious to the life that lay ready to ambush them the day after their graduation ceremony.

Olivia picked up the card again involuntarily. She read it closely now, analysing every bland, bubbly sentence for something to explain why Sharon had written her a postcard as if they were still friends. But there was nothing. The usual cheery emptiness of postcards. Great weather, beautiful sights, wonderful time, day trip to the Napa Valley, see you soon, lots of love, Sharon. See you soon was a bit rich, Olivia thought. God knows she'd tried to stay in touch, but it was Sharon who was always busy, stuck at work or struck down with a mystery illness when they were supposed to meet up for a meal in Covent Garden. Lots of love she could understand, even after so many years, but see you soon? She put the card down and went to make a cup of tea.

Sandra found the card waiting on her doormat when she got back from work. At first, glancing at the familiar word-processed address label, she thought it was from her parents, and as she poured herself a welcome-home gin and tonic she struggled to remember in which weekly phone call she had been informed about a trip to California.

As she sank into her armchair and flicked on the television, she looked at the card again and this time noticed the curly blue handwriting poking out from beneath the stern black type of her parents' laser printer. On the television a policeman was appealing for anyone with information on a white Ford Transit to come forward. She stared at the screen, letting the card hang limply in her hand, but the policemen's words were a blur. She thought vaguely about the curly blue writing and the white Ford Transit while planning an email she needed to send to the sales team in the morning and scouring the remembered image of her refrigerator for anything appetising that could be cooked in less than five minutes in the single clean pot she had available.

Sandra poured another gin and gulped it down. Nothing made sense. Numbers were appearing on the screen now. The West Midlands Police. Crimestoppers. Please come forward. Anonymity. White Ford Transit. Sharon. Who the hell was Sharon? No information came forward, anonymously or otherwise. Were you in the vicinity of Wimbledon Common in the early hours of Wednesday, 18th April? Sandra had no idea. She did remember something though: a chicken tikka masala on the second shelf of the fridge, just behind the multi-pack of vanilla yoghurts that she hadn't started yet. She left the woman being raped on Wimbledon Common and went to the kitchen to see if the chicken tikka was past its 'best before' date.

She really should have sent that email to the sales team before leaving, but it had been past eight o'clock and her brain had reached the point at which additional shots of sludge from the coffee machine failed to spark it into life. Tomorrow, then, but what would she say? The phone rang. She reached for the receiver, then realised she still had the card in her hand, and pinned it to the fridge with a pink breast cancer awareness magnet. That reminded her about the chicken tikka. She opened the fridge door, cradling the phone between her ear and shoulder and saying hello as she moved aside the yoghurt.

'Oh, hi, Olivia,' she said absent-mindedly. 'Long time no speak.' Only two days left to eat eight yoghurts. Not a good start. 'Fine, thanks, how are you?' The chicken tikka had expired three days ago, but on the other hand it had been in the back of the fridge and was covered with a thin layer of ice. Maybe it would be all right. 'Postcard? Yeah, I did get one. Was it from you?' She peeled back the plastic film and sniffed. Chemicals, with a hint of curry: nothing too bacterial. It would probably be fine if she heated it an extra thirty seconds. She closed the door, and saw the postcard wedged under the breast cancer magnet.

'Wait, Olivia,' she said. 'This postcard is from Sharon? University Sharon?'

'That's what I've been telling you for the last five minutes,' said Olivia huffily.

'But, I haven't ….'

'Neither have I.'

' … in twenty years now. Does she say anything on yours?'

'No. Yours?'

'No. It's as if nothing had happened.'

They were both silent. Olivia was the first to speak. 'Do you think we should ….'

'Yes. But I don't know where ….'

'Me neither.'

'Last I had was her parents' address, and I don't even know if I still have that.'

'Or if they still live there.'

'Yes. Stupid idea, I suppose.'

'I mean, she knows how to get in touch with us ….'

'Yes, she does.'

' … if she wants to say anything more than that it's sunny in California.'

'Yes.'

'Well, my dinner's almost cooked. I should go.'

'So late?'

'We're not all perfect housewives, Olivia.'

Silence.

'I'm sorry, that was ….'

'It's okay. Go and eat.'

'Okay. Bye then.'

The third postcard arrived at the house of a young couple in Darlington who studied it for a few moments, then threw it in the bin. Their landlord had given them a forwarding address for the previous tenants, but anyone before that was not their problem. They did, however, decide to go to California on their holidays that summer, if they could afford it.

The fourth and final postcard dropped through the letterbox of a 1930s semi-detached house on the outskirts of Manchester. Jean switched off the radio as soon as she heard the clang of the letterbox. She reached for her walking stick. Letters were rare these days as her friends died off and her few remaining family members seemed to have forgotten how to communicate without the aid of a gadget. Even the junk mail had dried up after she turned seventy, the building societies and glazing companies evidently having decided that she would not live long enough to provide a decent return on their second-class stamp. As for bills, she knew by heart the days on which they arrived, and there was nothing due today. Besides, she knew the sound of a bill flopping on the mat, and even over the radio chatter she could tell this was no bill. She'd heard it dancing lightly onto the carpet while the metal flap, meeting no resistance from bulky bills, slammed quickly back into place, probably giving the postman's finger a nasty pinch. This was a postcard, no doubt about it.

Jean shuffled to the door. The clock started chiming eleven as she was moving down the hall. The post was so late these days, she thought. No wonder people used computers instead. She reached the mat, gratified to see the postcard lying there, proving that her hearing was as acute as ever and that, as she tirelessly explained to everyone from solicitous nephews to condescending social workers, there was really no need for everyone to speak to her so loudly and slowly. She picked it up, walked back to the living room and settled into her chair by the window. She savoured the picture for several minutes: a wide-open desert landscape with a dead-straight road stretching off towards the blue sky. The words 'Road Trip USA' were emblazoned across the top, the big block letters filled with the stars and stripes of the American flag.

She was really rather pleased at the odd choice of card. Usually people sent her cards depicting some 'gentle' watercolour scene that they thought an old lady would like: ducks bobbing on a pond, sailing boats or, worst of all, flowers. This unusual image fired her imagination. She had never been to America, although she had always dreamed of it. There were rumours that her first husband had gone there after his National Service, and she often wanted to fly over there, find him and tell him that he was not the only one who had wanted to escape from the Manchester suburbs, to start a new life outside the stifling net-curtained world they'd grown up in. But instead she'd remarried, fenced herself in again, and consigned those wide American vistas to the realm of furtive imagination.

The clock chimed the quarter-hour, bringing her back to the present. She turned the card over, and when she saw the addressee she stopped breathing for a few seconds. Quickly reaching for her pills, she popped a couple on her tongue and swilled them down with some cold tea from the cup she'd abandoned earlier in the morning. She felt better instantly, the comforting familiarity of the pills in her throat taking effect long before the chemicals. With equilibrium restored, she sat for long minutes staring at the postcard. Then, when the clock chimed the half-hour, she rose slowly to her feet, shuffled across to her battered old mahogany bureau, sat down with a pad of Basildon Bond writing paper, her favourite black fountain pen and her daughter's pink address book, and started writing.

Sharon picked up the phone, started dialling the number, then hesitated. She read the letter again.

'As painful as it is for me to write letters like this, it still brought joy to an old woman's heart to know that her daughter is remembered by her friends.'

She couldn't call. Call and say what? You're crazy? I never sent your daughter a card. I haven't seen her, haven't wanted to see her, in twenty years?

She read the letter again. 'If you have any questions about Alice or how she passed away, please don't hesitate to call me.' It was pleading, almost, for someone to remember her Alice, to care about her. And Sharon did want to know. She still saw Alice as a party-loving twenty-one-year-old, always on the arm of some boy, always ready with the full giggling details for her friends later on. And Sharon remembered her mother, too. She must have had Alice late, because she seemed old even then, more like Alice's granny than her mother, and Sharon remembered the warm, calorie-filled welcome she always provided whenever her daughter had visitors.

It was her affection for the old lady that made Sharon hang up the phone. Let her enjoy her delusions. Sharon could live with the confusion of receiving a letter from nowhere about a postcard she'd never sent saying that a friend she hadn't seen in twenty years was dead.

She picked up the letter and scanned it again, just in case she'd missed anything. Still no clues. The formal style, 'I'm sorry to have to inform you …' smacked of a letter written many times before, to friends, distant relatives, banks. Only in the final paragraph was there a personal touch:

'I do hope that you enjoyed your "Road Trip USA" and am sorry to be the bearer of such bad news on your return.'

Odd choice of words for an old lady. Then suddenly in her mind an image of the postcard appeared. A wide expanse of sunbathed desert, a road stretching to the horizon, the words 'Road Trip USA' in red, white and blue across the top. Sharon shook her head. That was impossible. She hadn't been to the States since ….

Suddenly memories flooded her mind. America, San Francisco, the friends she'd stayed with in the Mission District, the motel room, the sleazy bar that she'd gone to after arguing with her parents on the phone, her visceral desire for revenge and escape, the way Bobby had approached her with a cheap beer and a cheap pickup line but she'd gone with him anyway out of spite at her cloistered, dead-end life; the way he'd whisked her off in his car, speeding down dark highways into the desert, the cool night air rushing in through the open windows, Dire Straits playing at full volume on the cheap crackling radio, her stifling English friends a world away and the thrill of her American adventure mingling with a rising fear of the unknown. Was he a criminal? A bank robber? A serial killer? Would he lock her in the trunk or chop up her yearning, unfulfilled body with a chainsaw and dump it in the vast expanse of black empty desert that whizzed by at 90 miles an hour just beyond the thin strip of white neon highway?

In the end it was safe enough. Cheap motels, greasy diners, dollar-a-bottle dark smoky bars, booze and pot, music and sex, sex and stories. Bobby was a born storyteller. He was never happier than when he was sitting at a table with a drink in his hand and an attentive audience listening to him ramble his way through some made-up, convoluted tale, laughing in all the right places, staying with him through the twists and turns, never pointing out any of the myriad contradictions.

Letting the old woman's letter fall to the table, Sharon hurried upstairs and pulled out the ladder from behind the wardrobe. She climbed up into the loft and rummaged around through clouds of dust until she found, under folders of unread university notes and ancient textbooks, a pink photo album with 'California 1987' printed on the front in the ridiculous embossed letters of her mother's ancient Dymo label maker. She dusted it off, covering her mouth with her forearm as the clouds of grime engulfed her. Then she backed away, climbed down, hurried to her bedroom, sat on the big, soft, double bed and opened it.

The first few shots were as anonymous as postcards. The Golden Gate Bridge, the Presidio, grand old buildings that she couldn't name any more: all the sights that a good tourist should capture. Then there were a few snaps of her friends Donny and Sarah, their dingy Mission District apartment just above what they called the 'Laundromat', their cute little hyperactive Jack Russell whose name Sharon was very disappointed not to remember.

Then suddenly things changed. The crowded San Francisco scenes gave way to photos of empty highways, diners, truck stops, small towns clinging to the road for protection from the desert and mountains beyond, huge redwood trees as far as the camera could see, the flat blue of the Pacific Ocean going all the way to Japan. And motels, endless motels, all different yet exactly the same.

She flicked through the pages impatiently until finally she found the picture she'd really been looking for. There was Bobby, leaning on the hood of his car, smoking a cigarette and trying to look like James Dean. Never mind that it was 1987 and he was leaning on a dented, rusty brown Nissan Maxima, wearing faintly preppy khakis and laughing too much to look like a rebel without a cause. Bobby still insisted that he looked like James Dean and, in a strange way, he did. He was not tall, but quite muscular, and his slightly pock-marked face did look slightly haunted sometimes, particularly when the bright early morning light accentuated the circles under his eyes from the night before. No matter how bad the hangover, he always made sure his mousy hair was gelled upwards in a slightly wavy, almost out of control Jimmy Dean fashion, and no matter how hot the California sun beat down, he never took off his weathered old leather jacket. But the laughter was always a problem. Bobby enjoyed life too much to be convincing in his hate-the-world act. His face could be arranged into a world-weary scowl only with effort; it looked much more natural creased into a warm smile as he told another inane joke or long-winded story or playfully mocked her 'aristocratic' English accent. Yet Bobby could not, or would not, let himself fully enjoy life. At some deep level it scared him greatly.

Sharon asked him once, sitting in some diner or other on some anonymous strip of road, what his name was. 'Bobby,' he replied. 'You forgotten already?'

'No. I mean your full name.'

He scratched his chin. 'My full name. Now you realise this is quite a commitment. I mean, this is like getting married or something.'

'Stop playing for time.'

'All right, all right. My full name is …' (and he used his knife and fork to make a dramatic drumroll on the sticky coffee-and-ketchup-stained table, causing the good folk on the next table to turn and stare) 'Robert Charles Ray McGee

Junior.'

Sharon giggled. 'Seriously? Bobby McGee. Like in the Janis Joplin song?'

'Oh, you know that song? Well, in that case my name's James Dean.'

'I've heard of him too.'

'Oh. Tom Cruise?'

And Sharon laughed and poked him in the chest, and he motioned to her to come and sit next to him in the booth, and they cuddled up and kissed and looked into each other's eyes and stroked each other's faces, letting their meatloaf and coffee get cold and congealed on the table in front of them and causing the good folk at the next table to forgo dessert and ask for the check, making some pointed remark to the waitress about being put off their food, at which the waitress shrugged and Sharon and Bobby sniggered. She called him 'Tom' for the next few days until it began to feel silly, and then she went back to 'Bobby', but that didn't feel right either.

She kept asking him what his real name was, but he grinned and joked and said that mystery was good in a relationship, which was true up to a point. But after a couple of months of zigzagging aimlessly around California highways in various states of intoxication, Sharon wanted to know something about the man she was with. Was he an artist? A convict? An escaped investment banker? All of these questions he answered in the affirmative, telling her a dozen different intricate and intensely plausible life stories. And she couldn't help laughing, but then she couldn't help wanting to know the truth, and asking more urgently, more seriously, every time.

'Don't you want more than this?' she said one night in a dingy motel room in Eureka. They were both in a bad mood, having driven around for hours trying to find a room, only to be told twenty times that it was July the Fourth weekend and everything had been booked up for months. Finally they'd found a $10-a-night flophouse on the edge of town, the kind of place where the owner sits nervously in a booth behind bulletproof glass and you hand your cash through a slot just large enough to accommodate dollar bills but narrow enough to keep out knives, guns and needles. Once they'd settled down in their room and killed as many beetles as they could, they desperately wanted something to lift their spirits. But Bobby said he was out of drugs, and didn't feel like going driving around in the dark trying to find a dealer or even a liquor store in this god-forsaken neon-light fairground-attraction family holiday town from hell. So they just lay on the lumpy bed, staring at the ceiling, with nothing to do other than replay the same old scene, with Sharon chasing and Bobby evading.

'I thought you were having a good time,' he said wearily.

'I am. But what happens next?'

Bobby chuckled bitterly. 'It always comes to this. What next? What next? What do you want next? Let me guess, a station wagon and a nice house in Weehawken, New Fucking Jersey, right?' His voice rose, reaching a crescendo on the 'Jer' of Jersey.

'Well, at least now I know what state you're from,' Sharon said. It was meant as a half-joke, but it sent Bobby purple with rage. 'I'm sorry, baby, I'm sorry,' she said hastily. 'It's just that I want to know something about the man I'm falling in love with. Just something. Doesn't have to be much. A name, a place, a job. Something.'

Bobby's ugly colour faded, his easygoing smile returned. 'That's sweet, baby,' he said. 'I love you too. We're just tired and cranky from all that driving around. Let's try to relax a little, huh?' And he turned out the light and they kissed in the semi-darkness, headlights occasionally flashing across their semi-naked bodies through the flimsy curtains. And soon feelings took over from thoughts and Sharon didn't care any more who Bobby was or where they were going or whether he really loved her. All she wanted was the moment, and as always when they were drunk or high or making love, she felt as if she understood him.

She was awake when he left in the morning. She heard the door sliding open and then gently being pushed shut, heard the car judder to life outside. She didn't feel surprise, or anger, or betrayal. She felt nothing, numb, used up, and was sure in the certainty of youth that she would never feel anything again as long as she lived. She got up from the bed and saw that he'd left a pile of crumpled five-dollar bills on top of the TV, enough for something to eat and a bus back to her friends in San Francisco. She pulled some clothes on, leaving the cheap ring he'd bought her in the drawer along with the cheery postcards that didn't seem worth sending now, and went out into the grey half-light of the morning to find a diner.

Sharon heard keys in the lock downstairs. California vanished. Guiltily she slid the album under her bed like a pornographic magazine. She got up, smoothed the covers, smoothed her hair, composed her face and went to kiss her husband, a good, decent man, not a great story-teller but the kind of man who could be relied upon, who told you his real name, the type who would put stamps on a stranger's postcards if he found them lounging in a motel drawer. She kissed him longer than usual and was glad to have him home, and she fussed over him and appreciated him and told him she was so happy. But as the evening wore on and the television programmes flashed before them like headlights on a highway, her thoughts kept straying back to that young, happy-sad James Dean impersonator leaning on the hood of a Nissan Maxima, smoking a cigarette and laughing in the darkness under the bed.

Andrew Blackman

Andrew Blackman is thirty years old and lives in north London. He recently moved back to the UK after spending six years in New York, where he worked as a staff reporter for the Wall Street Journal. He has also written for newspapers and magazines across America, including Monthly Review, the Cincinnati Post, Pittsburgh Post-Gazette, Seattle Times and Tampa Tribune, and won the Daniel Singer essay prize. He has a Bachelor's degree in modern history from Oxford University and a Master's degree in journalism from Columbia University.

You're Dead

When Peterson was sent upstairs he was meant to go and pack, but now he's out on the roof and nobody knows what to do. The teachers are all standing around on the grass looking confused, and the Head is holding a megaphone to his beard and shouting upwards.

The voice rebounds off the building and echoes across the field towards the woods.

Then the first black square comes spinning down through the inky-blue sky and explodes on the path, showering the lawn with stones. Teachers murmur nervously. The Head squats down and picks up a piece of tile shrapnel. He turns it over and over in his hand. He doesn't know what to do next. I bet he regrets not sending someone to supervise Peterson with the packing.

The Head stands up again, and shouts louder.

'Matthew Peterson, you are going to be in a lot of trouble for this!'

The megaphone sings a long, high note of static, which chases after the yell. The next tile flies right past the Head's head and shatters on the gravel.

What the teachers don't know, but I see perfectly from here, is that Peterson is also flinging tiles down the other side of the building, into the staff car park. He knows his punishment can't get any bigger. The Head understands this too, and has run out of ideas.

It's getting dark; Peterson's mum will be here soon to collect him.

Peterson sleeps in the bed next to mine, but after today his'll be free. That's something I have been praying for since my first week.

Once, in 3A, I found some boys cutting the heads off Peterson's soldiers with a Stanley knife. I knew straight away there'd be trouble and wanted nothing to do with it. I even said to them all, 'I am nothing to do with this.'

They all looked at me as if I was the one being stupid. I left. But then someone lied and told Peterson it was me, 'cause later on in the upstairs corridor I saw Peterson marching towards me, angrier than I have ever seen him before. His face was the colour of Ribena. He was staring straight at me as he got closer and muttered 'You're dead' through his teeth without moving his lips. When he ran at me I couldn't move. I just stood there saying 'Wait …' and 'But …' like questions. And when his fist hit my mouth I crumpled to the floor and held my lips closed around my bleeding teeth. I cried not from pain but because I hadn't done anything.

Later on, Peterson and I had had to stand in the Head's room for hours, waiting for Peterson to say sorry. The Head just shuffled piles of paper around on his desk and did marking. He was ready to sit there all night. We were in there so long that I had time to memorise all the authors and titles on the Head's bookshelves, and I hadn't even heard of any of them. Peterson spent the whole time looking out of the window. Finally, when even the Year Sixes were in bed, Peterson said sorry. He was still looking out of the window when he said it so it shouldn't've counted, but I think the Head was getting tired by then because he just nodded to himself then told us to go to bed.

Just as I was falling asleep a fist thumped into my belly, and I lay in the dark gulping for air, blinking away hot tears, desperate not to make any sound at all.

The tiles are still falling when Peterson's mum arrives. Someone hears the car in the drive and goes to explain where her son is. She comes around the side of the building just as another tile comes cartwheeling through the sky. This time it stabs into the lawn and stays there, upright, like a shark's fin swimming through a sea of grass.

Mrs Peterson looks even angrier than the Head. She snatches the megaphone from his hand and tries to shout through it, but nothing comes out.

'How do you work this fucking thing?' she snaps at the Head, and he shows her how to pull the trigger to make your voice come out. This time the shout works.

'Matthew? Matthew, do you hear me? I have driven for three bloody hours to get here. If you think I want to play games with you then you've got another thing coming. You have one minute to get down here, before I come up there and throw you down.'

Peterson is sitting on the peak of the roof. The sky has just enough blue light left in it for him to be a silhouette. He doesn't say anything back, but at least the tiles have stopped falling.

Then I see the sitting figure stand and clamber down the slope of the roof to the edge.

What happened is this. Everybody else had the swimming competition today, but I was allowed to go out in the field because I had a verucca.

I was near the summer house when I heard shouts coming from the woods. Nobody else was off-games, so whoever was in there shouldn't've been.

I couldn't tell how many voices there were but one of them was definitely Peterson. That was weird because I knew Peterson was meant to be doing front crawl. Peterson has the record for two lengths. He's never off-games, and always wins the swimming competition.

So I started walking towards the woods to investigate, but I didn't hurry. If you've got any brains, when Peterson shouts you run away. But something about this shout made me go towards it.

As I walked across the field I could see everyone up by the pool. Chlorine floated down and mixed with the smell of cut grass. I could hear the dives hitting the water and girls' screams as high as Miss T's whistle. The sun was out over the school roof and warmed one side of my face. There hadn't been any clouds for days.

Close to the woods the grass is long because the branches are too low for Mr Way's tractor. Mr Way's job is to look after all the grass. He is always rolling it and mowing it, sometimes even talking to it. He has a page in the school magazine called 'Thoughts on Grass' where he tells us about the grass and whether or not it had a good term.

I walked along the edge of the trees looking into the woods but I didn't see anyone. The shouts had stopped, so I thought whoever had been there had gone. But then deep inside the woods I saw something blue flapping and heard crying noises. The boys' uniforms are snooker-table green; the girls wear dresses the colour of a baby boy's blanket. So I knew it was a girl.

I couldn't see who it was because her head was turned but I could see she was tied to a tree.

I ran in, and when I got close I could see it was Gemma. She was shaking so hard she couldn't speak. You could tell she had been crying but she had stopped, and tracks of salt had dried on her face where the tears had run down. The shoelaces had burned purple lines across her wrists and ankles, and the knots were tiny and tight. They got tighter when I tried to snap the laces. I had to use my teeth, even though they always tell us that our teeth are for eating with and nothing else.

Straight away Gemma ran off and I could hear she was crying again. I shouted after her.

'Was it him?'

She didn't answer me, but I already knew it was.

She kept running, fast towards the Lecky block, and I followed across the field. Everyone was still splashing and swimming and nobody seemed to notice or care that we weren't up there cheering with them. Gemma ran into the Lecky block and when I caught up with her she had gone into the French room. I asked her again if it was Peterson and she just told me to go away.

'I know it was him,' I insisted. 'I heard his voice.'

'GO AWAY,' she screamed.

I stood around outside. After a while I opened the Lecky door again but I couldn't walk in. The door swung back closed, and my shutting reflection looked like a hologram as it came back to face me.

I walked back up the steps towards school. Inside, the long corridor was dark and smelt of varnish. Crowd cheers bounced through the open windows and along the empty walls, down to the Head's door at the end.

I don't like telling, but rules change when it's something big.

In total I have had to stand in the Headmaster's study five times. But when I went in there to tell him about Gemma, that was the first time I had ever been in there on my own.

I knocked on the door. I heard a chair squeak and then the Head groaned, 'Come in'.

I told him about Gemma and the shoelaces. Then I told

him about Peterson's shouts in the woods.

Behind the Head, through the window, I could see that there were people in the pool, but that the races had stopped and people were doing bombs off the diving board. He asked me some more questions and then said thank you, which means get out.

In my head, Peterson muttered, 'You're dead'.

I went back down to Lecky. Gemma was still in the French room and would only let Matron near. Matron came to the door when she saw me. The upside-down clock safety-pinned to the top pocket of her shirt reflected the sun into my face. She told me I wasn't needed and went back inside.

Matron is big and laughy and has a nickname for almost everyone. Once I called her 'Mummy' by accident but she just laughed.

I walked back to the woods and threw stones at the tree, imagining it was his face, and I only rested when I heard people coming. I realised I was crying too, but the realising made me stop.

It was Miss T and Mr Potter. Mr Potter knelt down and felt the marks on the bark with his hairy fingers. They looked like fat caterpillars exploring the tree trunk. He was shaking his head lots. Miss T told me to go in. I stayed outside in the long grass. They were only in the woods for a few minutes and when Miss T came out the lenses of her glasses changed colour and became sunglasses, hiding her eyes. Mr Potter followed, and when he stepped into the sunlight I saw millions of tiny ginger hairs in his beard that I had never noticed before. Normally his beard is the colour of mud.

I heard the bell ring but the thought of food brought a sick taste to my mouth.

Mr Potter and Miss T started walking back towards school. I followed them, but hid behind the tree on the lawn and looked into the Head's study. I could see Chapman and he was crying. When I leaned over I could see past the curtain, and that's when I saw Peterson, smirking like he'd just farted. I've never seen him cry. The Head was talking into the telephone. None of them could see me. I wished as hard as I could that Peterson would go, before I became the sneak.

A car engine started down by Lecky and I ran. Gemma was wrapped in a red blanket and put in the back of the white car that's always parked there. Matron got in the front. The car bumped up the hill and Gemma held up her palm at me in a wave. I waved back, slowly closing my hand as the car drove away. Then I walked out across the field. The sun was coming down behind the school and made the sky behind look like a bruise. Kip was alone on the other side of the field, digging for something. Mr Way was by the pavilion hammering something metal, and the noises came a long time after each hit. The three of us were a triangle, and in the middle the shadows of trees were a hundred meters long.

When they found out that Peterson was up on the roof the teachers sent everyone to bed, even though it was still early. They've let me stay out here on the wall by the pool because I am something to do with this.

Kip has come up from the woods because she heard all the loud voices, and she's lying near me chewing on something she dug up. Mr Way is over with the teachers, who are all interrupting each other trying to explain what has happened.

I'm not sure if Gemma will be back. Chapman has already gone home. He went upstairs straight away to pack all his things, and didn't go out on the roof to throw tiles.

When Peterson was standing on the edge of the roof

he looked down at the ground as if he was about to jump. A secret part of me willed him to. I know it's wrong but I wished him to slip and break his neck, but he didn't.

Now he comes out through the back door and walks across the lawn towards his mum. The teachers sigh in unison, relieved that no more people got hurt. Peterson's mum snaps at him, 'Now get in the car,' but he stops walking when he sees me.

For a second I think he's coming this way, that he's going to punch me in the face again for being a sneak. Instead he gobs on the grass between us, then turns and carries on walking. And like that, the bed beside mine becomes empty.

Now that the excitement is over, the teachers have gone back inside school. I'm sitting on the wall in the dark, with Kip still lying near my feet. She gets up and follows when I walk over the lawn, and watches as I wrestle the embedded tile out of the turf.

The surface of the pool is tight like cling film; the water is so still you cannot even tell there is any. The tile sluices the surface and sinks. Waves bounce off the sides, echoing and overlapping, as the dark shape sinks beneath.

Tom Williams

Tom Williams lives and writes in London.